A HOT DATE WITH WITH DESTINY

A HOT DATE WITH DESTINY

A Novel By

Richard Chandler Burroughs

A HOT DATE
WITH
DESTINY

Acknowledgements

I would like to thank all of my friends and family whose zaniness, fears, joy, obsessions, love and life gave me the content for the words in this novel.

I would like to thank my mother for being my mom, for being a loving and caring person. Always there for me no matter what!

I Dedicate this to my Grandmother with whom, from time to time, I would have silent conversations about writing, staying locked onto a goal and a dream, even when that dream becomes somewhat deferred. I Hope that she isn't looking down and blushing over the content. ☺

TABLE OF CONTENTS

Prologue: Page 6

Chapter 1: Page 13

Chapter 2: Page 23

Chapter 3: Page 39

Chapter 4: Page 59

Chapter 5: Page 81

Chapter 6: Page 93

Chapter 7: Page 102

Chapter 8: Page 120

Chapter 9: Page 133

Chapter 10: Page 152

PROLOGUE

All of the dirty talk in the cab had gone to hell. The saucy conversation was great; it was all about body parts wet, perky and hard as granite. The game was called dirty cab ride, which, is a full two-steps past foreplay and a step before some push and pull action; and he was the filthy tour director. He rode the fluctuations of the road so that his mouth flitted a flash of flesh and found her tenderness with his five free fingers, while the other five, for the record, were jammed down the back of her skintight jeans.

With muted moaning they moved towards a destination that was east. All he could get out was that they were going east and then he had the most wonderful nipple between his lips. After a few blocks of clueless driving, he lifted his head and told Senõr Cabbie to take them to the W hotel in Union Square but quickly buried his head back into her décolleté and suckled like an infant. The cab pulled over as he rustled through his pocket for cash while fingering a lighter, bag of pot, credit and debit card, business card, metro card, other people's business cards and something that felt like a bullet.

The doorman for the W opened the cab door on the curbside and out popped little miss B cup with a slight wobble. Austin tipped the Cabbie extra for allowing such a carnal experience to happen on his shift and then stumbled towards the elevator with debauched laughter and a sense of waiting pleasure. He fingered his pocket again and remembered that he left his card key in the room and proceeded to the front desk to get a replacement.

Coincidence would place a familiar face behind the counter, attached to an acquaintance named Josh. After a very quick acknowledgement he darted his eyes over to the elevator bank, peeked at the girl, looked back at Austin and gave a subtle smile. Now, with card key firmly in hand he pressed for the elevator when his heart sank! The by-product of his carnal cab moment, besides sticky fingers, was his entrance into the weed-less zone; he left his pot in the goddamn cab.

It gnawed at his nerves that he still had a serious problem when it came to keeping track of his belongings. It plagued him since childhood. As a wee boy, he would lose the usual menagerie of gloves, hats, mittens, umbrellas, notebooks and any other item not stapled to his calf muscle, though he fully believed he would grow out of it. He chalked it up to being a careless kid. Austin hoped it was a problem that, ironically, you lose, when you become an adult. He figured if he began to like broccoli and spinach, as he got older, then he would surely turn into a man who kept track of his possessions.

That magical transformation had yet to happen and in the interim he was still losing all kind of items such as pot, digital cameras (2), cell phones (10+), hats, scarves, watches (2) and even a friend's dog (long story). Still, he hadn't lost track of the amazing arrangement of tits, lips, legs, hair and other supple body parts staring at him as they boarded the elevator. The door hadn't completely closed yet when she pounced on him like an un-caged animal.

She struggled to kiss Austin as he pulled her away from his face by her hair. It was like watching the Discovery Channel as she stuck her freshly pierced tongue out to touch his mouth and the more he pulled her face away, the more she strained. He released her hair and the momentum flung them together, lips meeting, heads banging, bodies becoming one. When he grabbed the girl by the neck and pushed her backwards into the corner of the elevator, he felt a sensation.

Austin had his hand pressed up against her throat in a very certain way and though not causing any marks, he was choking her with a bit of force. It wasn't a "Boston Strangler" but his grip was *just* firm enough to spark a minimum level of fear. He tightened his grip a little more and nibbled her ear as he whispered into it "mi loco mami", which, tragically, was nearly the extent of his Spanish.

At that point Austin was sure that a small light bulb flicked on in the back of the girls head, illuminating how she really didn't know him. What if Austin was some kind of killer? A bonafide mass murderer with "based on a true story" tattooed across his chest and she was his next victim. What if she wound up being "found" by the police, bound and gagged and very dead? Before that thought could gather much steam, her raging libido kicked back in and she unzipped his pants with a sultry smile; and he didn't even know that sultry was possible by an eighteen year old.

Austin's room was on the eighteenth floor. On the tenth floor a very obvious escort service girl entered the elevator and asked if they were going up. Austin, being lust drunk and a bit stoned, shook his head and pointed down. When the elevator doors shut and the car went up, escort girl shot Austin a dirty look like he was being an asshole. Then she looked at eighteen year old and cursed the existence of sexy, young girls that were horny, drunk and ready to screw. That's why the whore hates the hoe; because the hoe could put the whore outta business!

The eighteen-year old and Austin exited the elevator and made their way down the corridor, turning left instead of right and tried sticking the card in the wrong door. They doubled back, corrected their course and whispered loudly about a variety of crazy shit. All inhibitions were out the window as her sweet little mouth released the dirtiest possible thoughts.

Austin spun her around on his back as her hot breath warmed his neck and left a moist residue of bottle service vodka cranberries. She thumped the hallway walls with her feet, surely jolting awake many of the early rising business travelers on the eighteenth floor and probably scared a few people in the process.

Perhaps it was the dervish piggyback ride and had nothing to do with karma coming back to bite him, but as Austin slid the card key in and out of the slot, the eighteen year old suddenly looked quite woozy. She was wearing that unmistakable face of someone that was about to throw up and then, wham, once inside the door, she was gagging violently. She was gagging up all the potential of the night.

"This is not right, this is all wrong….the only gagging she should be doing is on the animal bulging behind my zipper" Austin thought. He rushed her into the bathroom just in time as she started hurling while in descent towards the toilet bowl, which she began hugging like a small baby to a mother's bosom. If you've never had the pleasure of this experience, let it be known that it's soooo un-sexy; like diarrhea at a pool party. It was the worst situation!

Without warning-well there was a two or three second warning before she shit her guts out through her mouth- the night had morphed into a really bad story. It was a sad, tragic and painful end of a night that was just about to get interesting. The ramrod erection he was sporting, courtesy of his very first Viagra pill, was all dressed up with nowhere to go. The worst part was he had turned into a caregiver, a freakin' night nurse, if you will. He was holding up the girl's head so she didn't choke on her vomit. She was dribbling creamed corn down his shirtsleeve and babbling about how sorry she was for getting so drunk.

Austin knew the girl's name, although he'd been saying it wrong all night. He was bad with names, which always sounded like pretentious bullshit, and on top of that, the girl's name was really hard to pronounce. Toss in numerous drinks with loud music and you had a recipe for lots of pronouns and terms of endearment. He must have called her everything short of her name, including sweetie, baby, shorty, and cupcake, lovely and even sweet cheeks. At one point he even called her Yo.

He met her just a few hours earlier but Austin couldn't kick her out. Although he may have been mad that she'd ruined his shirt, his trainers and soiled the toilet, Austin was really cool with a bunch of her friends and they would never let him live it down. Besides, he wasn't that cold of a dude.

The dude he was previously would have gone into her pocket book, removed her credit card and switched it with his at the front desk. Then he would have ordered tons of room service, watched some pay per view porn and jacked off in her hair while she slept off her stupidity; and he would have smiled while doing it.

But he changed and became a bit more humane, though it was the frickin' "humanity" that had stuck him with a really hot eighteen year old chic hugging what turned into an unsanitary toilet bowl in a hotel bathroom. Damn! Ready for some action had turned into nothing but babble. Ridiculous, x-rated babble! *We pre-empt this promising sex jump-off with a special bulletin from somewhere in the back of your mind- "wine is fine but liquor is quicker, though too much of either and it's bye-bye beaver!*

CHAPTER 1

It was summertime in the wonderful place called New York City yet the CSI team would have been hard pressed to turn up any telltale signs. The archenemy was the weather, since it made leaving the house quite the daunting task. Dressing properly for the day was extremely difficult when the weather flip-flopped like a politician wooing swing state votes. There were way too many moments between the mirror and weather.com, while peeking out the window to see if other people were dressed like it was fall or summer.

The choice was eventually one of the many pairs of Levi's shrink to fit jeans that he never washed, so they never shrunk. It was reminiscent of the three weeks that Austin had recently spent in South Beach, Miami. Sex, sand and pot; how good it would be to go back to that he thought. He was surely living in the wrong city, if for nothing else but the existence of winter. It would simplify his life if dressing in the morning was nothing more than a T-shirt, a pair of jeans and some flip-flops.

At that moment he was on the cusp of running late for a meeting. As always, he was on the cusp of running late for a meeting. He was on the cusp of catching a cab instead of the train, since he was on the cusp of running late and hell, he was actually on the cusp of losing his mind. He'd already lost direction. Completely. He was moving; yet it was more like drifting. Unsure and totally without purpose, just drifting. The whole feeling of not having any purpose sounded so cliché, and although he was opposed to a cliché existence, it ironically sounded cliché to say that something sounded "cliché".

It was as if the whole thing-the life that he lived-was a weird dream. It was the classic one, where he was trying to run while stuck in quicksand or some other metaphorical muck. It was the type of dream that was easily decoded by a random, truck-stop hooker or an Internet psychic. He was in his early thirties; he wasn't married and wasn't even close to getting hitched. He actually didn't feel that he was the marrying type anymore. He was hard to please and had very little trust of women, yet he really wanted to settle down with a hot little chic someday.

That was probably the problem! To be looking for a "hot little chic" at that point in his life was insane. He really should have had his eye open for a nice woman to settle down with. He actually needed help but, like a man driving to a family reunion out of state, he refused to ask for directions. He couldn't. He was resolute in self-determination even in situations where he could really have used a helping hand.

Cigarettes were a prime example. He was actually a smoking, anti-smoker. He always thought that smokers were stupid. A smoker singed their tongue with each tobacco stick turning people off, while keeping a bunch of corporate schmucks super-wealthy! He wouldn't get the patch and save his miserable life, but he hated smoking.

Austin always figured that he would have to quit cold turkey, which sounded cool and tough. Perhaps, that could explain its popularity as a method for kicking bad habits. If it were called warm pigeon, the whole act would lose much of its appeal Austin always thought. That being said, he was still keenly aware that he couldn't stop smoking for more than a few days of his own volition.

Actually, that wasn't the truth, since he once quit for three months; though that wasn't long at all, upon closer examination. That's a trimester in a woman's pregnancy, the length of a season, or the amount of time a pop song stays on Billboard's top 100. It was the equivalent of being the Brittney Spears of mental toughness.

Maybe that day was the day that he broke down and got the patch, especially since New York City had recently initiated a free patch give-away program. The odds on Austin actually following through on that, though, were small. It was circus sideshow small. If he did that, he might as well go all out and do several other things for the first time.

Perhaps he'd go to the newspaper stand and play lotto, even though he knew his chances of winning the lottery were worse than the chances of a snow cone surviving in hell. Austin didn't think that he fit the jackpot winner's profile since they all seemed to be of retiring age, recent immigrants or lunch pail carrying, blue collar workers; and he was none of the above.

Not that a profile determines the winner he thought, but there must be something about retirees, immigrants and blue collar workers and some sort of natural predisposition to picking the right numbers that just wasn't in his genes. The Levi shrink to fit pair; the ones that never shrunk because he never washed them. It essentially left him out of the power ball running, but there were still tons of things that he had yet to do.

Perhaps he would call an escort service and hire some chic named "Amber", but with his luck, he thought, it would be the same girl he ran into on the elevator of the W Hotel the night his dalliance with the eighteen year old came to an unhappy ending. For a series of four-minute companions he could go to scores and tip a harem of disinterested silicone princesses or maybe go to Hooters and order up some atomic wings from "Becky", the die-hard Mets fan with an autistic kid at home and ripe casaba melons under her shirt. Those thoughts made him laugh, but only as a distraction.

It was quite imperative for Austin to break the nicotine grip that cigarettes had on him. His mother quit smoking, aided by the patch, so he knew that it worked and appeared to be quite painless, which was supposedly the exact opposite of quitting cold turkey. He heard "cold turkey" stories where people were bed ridden, sweating like day laborers, suffering massive headaches, body aches and chills. That sounded like a masochist's wet dream, but a nightmare on Phlegm Street to Austin.

Actually, his mother and grandmother quit smoking with the patch at the same time but his grandmother still died from cancer at the young age of seventy-eight. His grandma was smoke free for maybe twenty years but still ended up a lung cancer victim, which didn't seem right. If she kept smoking, perhaps she would have been like one of those Old Russian women, still lighting up well into her nineties.

His grandmother's quality of life improved greatly after she kicked the butts, which was reason in itself to put down the Marlboros, he thought (or rather Benson & Hedges, which was her brand of choice). He figured if he stopped smoking now, he could live a long and miserable life, instead of one marked by misery and death at an early age.

While she was alive Austin and his grandmother had a quirky relationship. It had its nuances and was never a Norman Rockwell painting, yet there was absolute beauty in what they shared; love for food, dance and sports. As he watched his grandma die, which was a sad and surreal experience, it was almost like a movie, albeit a very sad Fellini matinee. It was sad because he would never see her again, which is a very simple yet powerful statement and surreal because he knew nothing about death.

One of the main characteristics separating humans from other animals is the awareness of being alive! Awareness of life makes it clear that death is sure and the end of the proverbial road. Still, Austin was also aware that humans only knew life. As a child, death was the one thing that was hardest to understand and the hardest to explain; well besides the whole caterpillar to butterfly thing. It's difficult for a child to wrap their head around the concept of death because death's definition wasn't simple and under a Snapple bottle cap.

Austin felt that no person, excluding a few nut jobs on the A Train, actually knew death or what it was like to be dead. For most folks, death was their biggest fear. He knew that if you snatched the "Jesus Freak" off the A train, stuffed him and his "Jesus Is Coming" sign into a trunk and popped it open behind Giants stadium in the Meadowlands that the trunk would reek of fear.

If you dragged the Jesus Freak out the trunk, slung him into the mud (there's always mud out there), stomped on his sign and put a piece of cold steel to his temple or in his mouth, like clockwork, he would beg for his life. Mind you, this was from the dude who walked around telling everybody that the world was about to end at any minute and that he was "Ready to Die"; though most people aren't so Notorious B.I.G. when it comes down to it.

So the smoking and his grandmother and the Jesus freak were in one big mental bubble, banging around his head while Austin dealt with the situation at hand, which was that he was running late. He finally solved his clothing dilemma and was now ready to head out the door and face the world. He stashed a pack of putrid smokes conveniently in the front and readily accessible part of his briefcase, and even as he walked out the door, he was keenly aware of falling into one of his favorite traps. It was playing out even though he would prefer that it didn't.

This was the scenario: He damned himself for running late, so he headed to the train instead of hailing a cab. He's disgusted about being late again and punished himself by taking the train. The self-imposed punishment only exacerbated the situation and made Austin later, which leads to him seething at his inability to arrive at anything in a timely manner.

His mother always said that he was going to be late to his own funeral and she's probably right, though his timely arrival at that appointment would be out of his hands. With his luck, Austin's hearse would surely be driven by tardy Ted, the inept driver who's the laughingstock of the funeral industry.

In his haste to catch the train Austin forgot to pick up a newspaper, which left him at the mercy of all the prying, insane subway eyes. He took a peek at the sports page that the dude next to him was reading but stopped when it became uncomfortable. It was actually a combination of that man's discomfort and Austin's sudden twinge of hypocrisy since he loathed people reading his paper from the next seat. He looked to lock his vision on anything to avoid eye contact, which was never easy to do.

Austin's glance towards the other side of the subway car turned up a jarring sight. The train was crowded and people were blocking his line of vision but Austin thought he spotted a friend of this asshole named Dillon, to whom Austin owed a three thousand dollar poker debt. Dillon's been talking shit about it, telling people he's looking for Austin, although Austin didn't think he was very hard to find. Austin was usually good with debt, not including student loans, library late fees, a credit card here and there and the occasional ex-girlfriend, but he vowed that debt would not get paid.

Again, it's not that he was against paying back his debts, but he was totally against being hustled. A three-card Monte shyster tragically victimized a teenaged Austin. It happened down on Broadway, in Greenwich Village, and the experience had left him damaged. It was money that he'd saved from working a crappy part-time job after school and he was en route to buy a drum kit that he'd had his eye on for months. Austin could have developed into a big time drummer for a famous band, a frequent bold-faced name in gossip columns; but noooooooooo-that guy had to hustle Austin out of his dreams and glory.

It was that card hustler's fault that Austin wasn't a drug addled party boy trying to revive his once glorified music career through Reality Television! Because of that, and a few other instances, Austin had a deep resentment towards being hustled. In that poker scam, Dillon colluded with several other people at the poker game to hustle Austin.

Their goal wasn't to hustle any mark they could find, but to hustle Austin specifically. Getting played like a chump wasn't cool and especially getting played like a chump by a chump like Dillon! Because of that he decided that the debt was bogus and he wasn't going to pay it.

The dossier on Dillon, cribbed for the sake of brevity, is that he was the bastard by-product of privileged upbringing and hip-hop culture. He was an upper eastside jerk with delusions of being a tough guy from the hood. He's what happens when hip-hop goes wrong, riding around in a shiny Range Rover, windows down, blasting the latest underground mix tape while blowing weed smoke out the sunroof.

He hung out with a group of doppelgangers that everyone called "The Dillons", much to the chagrin of the whole crew. They feigned as if they had their own identities, styles and ideas, yet this insistence when the contrary was obvious only escalated the absurdity, nee, the hilarity.

It appeared as if they got dressed in the morning during a video conference call that originated from Dillon's closet. The Dillons all towed the same opinions from politics to sports to Mac or PC. If you ever asked a question around them, they would wait until Dillon answered and then pipe in slightly different variations of his response. They were quite amusing and entertaining for a few minutes at a time, especially when those moments involved drugs or alcohol.

CHAPTER 2

The beginning of the Dillon/Austin conflict was rooted in a hot chic, which, famously, felled many an empire and presidential campaign. It was because of a girl that Dillon set up that poker game, marked the cards and fleeced Austin, or rather, tried to fleece Austin, out of the three grand. Dillon was, and still is, madly in love with this girl named Melissa and unfortunately for Dillon, she really didn't feel the same way about him.

Austin would often run into them at of the moment restaurants or lounges where Dillon was spending money like he made it in his basement. Melissa always looked disinterested and removed as Dillon was running a tab on his Amex black card, in what he surely assumed was an impressive gesture of affection. Austin knew him through a coterie of shared acquaintances, though they never had anything resembling an actual friendship.

He didn't have a real problem with Dillon prior to the whole Melissa situation, although Austin thought that Dillon's attitude was always a put off. Dillon acted as if god shitted him out and anointed him king of all he surveyed. He dropped names like a clumsy kid in pre-school, always out of context and in an effort to puff up his self worth.

Now, if you lived Austin's life, it was pretty common to run into a Dillon since they abound like UGG Boots and status handbags. Luckily, he'd become quite immune to that particular type of asshole. Perhaps, in an effort to clarify Dillon's personality, a list of some of the different types of assholes running around in the social scene would be useful:

DILLONS-See preceding paragraph

OPPORTUNITY KNOCKERS

This is the girl that, because she suddenly got a tit job, will only speak to people that offer her opportunities. If you could get her free drugs or bottles at clubs, take her on trips or keep her in the latest fashion, she's your friend to the end. The people she knew before visiting the plastic surgeon had to reapply for her friendship. She often starts going out before her knockers were healed and because she's a freak, it quickly becomes public knowledge that her tits look horrible.

LABEL SNOBS

This person is either a guy or a girl and they judge people on the fashion labels that they wear. It's not enough for someone to look stylish, these assholes need to know the designer and will judge a person based on *who* they're wearing. Sometimes they don't ask a person what designer they're wearing, they tell them what they're wearing since they know every designer's pieces on sight. They're quick to put someone on blast for wearing something from "Last Season's" collection.

FASHION VICTIMS

Different from Label Snobs, these people are "Johnny on the Spot" for any new and emerging fashion designer. They're boastful about wearing clothes from obscure artistes featuring bizarre functions. They'll whisper in your ear, while you're having cocktails and conversation, that they're wearing a jacket made of recycled, titanium infused wool, designed by a blind Mongolian monk and that it folds up into an incense holder or iPod case. If you ask where you could buy one, the label snob will blow you off by saying it's only sold at five boutiques world-wide but that theirs came straight from the design studio, or in this case, a cave in the Himalayas.

OVER TALKER
The over talker thinks that they have the end all statement,
opinion, witty comment or recent gossip and therefore tries
to dominate every conversation. Not so much a
conversation as a monologue, the over talker is in love with
their voice. It's easy to get trapped when "conversing" with
the over-talker because there's no way to excuse yourself
and step away. The best thing to do with an over-talker is to
invite another over talker into the conversation and escape
when they both start to smoke from the ears.

With that in mind, Dillon's pontification on the
beauty of a San Tropez beach in the winter or St. Bart
during holiday never bothered Austin. In fact, he found it
quite amusing whenever Dillon's spiel began to roll. The
few times that Dillon's act did become overbearing Austin
would simply bounce from the situation and leave it far
behind without harboring any residual feelings.
Still, Dillon was belligerent with his ability to be an
asshole and he wielded it like a blunt object found at a
crime scene. There was one instance, when he had
consumed a bit too much champagne, that Dillon said
something really awkward about immigrants and made
everyone, including Melissa and The Dillons, way
uncomfortable.
He must have thought himself quite the wit as his
smug laughter flew in the face of every offended party in
his company. It was at that moment that Austin really took
a good look at Melissa. He peeped around to see
everybody's reaction to Dillon's statement and noticed how
beautiful her eyes were.

Now, he wasn't trying to be overly poetic about the moment but her eyes had a sparkle of light that danced around like delicate ballerinas. They spoke to Austin of a longing for fulfillment in her life that was missing like WMD'S in Iraq. It was actually a combination of how her eyes looked and how they looked at him.

Her eyes cut through Austin's rough exterior. It cut through the scar tissue that was developed through years of dealing with bullshit, bull-shitters and from quite a bit of bullshitting himself. Melissa's eyes spoke directly to the remnants of love and humanity inside of Austin that was unsoiled by the world.

Nothing of any consequence happened that night between Melissa and Austin, as it was just a spark that lit a small, smoldering fire of possible destiny between the two. They basically had the hots for each other from that moment on or at least that's what Austin thought; but then again he voted Ralph Nader for president one year (though he did it on a drunken bet). He saw Melissa several times after that particular incident, but since he sported those old school values, he wouldn't even approach a woman if he knew that she was with someone else.

Austin suffered through repeated introductions to Melissa, common in social situations, and they subsequently established a running joke, shared between two people who were introduced far too many times yet didn't really know each other. They would shake hands and pretend that it was their first time meeting while fighting bursts of laughter:

Hey Austin, meet my friend Melissa, hey Melissa-do you guys know each other
Austin
"Yeah, I think we've met before-isn't your father an Oncologist?"

Melissa
"No, he's a zoo keeper-though oncology was his true love"
Austin
"Oh yeah, Oncology is the shit! -Well it's good meeting you again...its Melissa right?"

Then, like a wallet left unattended at a dive bar, she was gone and it wasn't until several months later that he would run into her again, and by that time Melissa's life had changed significantly. It was at a Yoga class that Austin unexpectedly eyed her lovely form again and oh what a site it was.

Austin would usually see Melissa sitting at a table, sipping on a cocktail or amongst a crowd of people or sometimes on the street in passing; but never in a skimpy, sweaty leotard holding an impossible position usually reserved for Cirque De Soleil performers. In a very dirty, BET Uncut sort of way, Austin was impressed with her flexibility. Mind you, that was only his second time attending the class so he was in the corner, taken aback with embarrassment at his rendition of the difficult positions. How he even ended up taking Yoga was not a conversion to new age idealism and principles.

He didn't become a Vegan and protest international trade agreements but was rather in dire need to lower his stress level; which was super high for a man his age. Austin was told that Yoga could help bring his stress levels down and also provide a better outlook on life. The latter part was a bit ambitious in describing Yoga's benefits Austin thought, but if it did that as well, he'd take it.

He cruised around checking for the ideal Yoga class and once he figured out that exact type of class didn't exist, Austin settled for one that was in his neighborhood. Austin's only concern was seeing people at the yoga class in such embarrassing positions, when he would also have to see them in the deli, pharmacy and laundromat.

Not that he was the easily embarrassed type, but he could get uncomfortable in certain situations. The proximity of the class to his apartment offered Austin the comfort of using his own shower after the class, and was the deal sealer, since he wasn't a big fan of showering at public facilities.

He was fifteen minutes into the yoga class when Austin first noticed her body. He wasn't trying to objectify her in the least, but he simply couldn't see her face with the position she was holding. All he saw was a protruding pelvis area, long, taut legs and a juicy little ass; and this was through the reflection in the mirror. He would catch the reflection with casually deceptive glances; as the only guy in a class full of women, the last thing Austin wanted to become was a leering letch. So he became a cautious leering letch!

He was sitting in a god fearing position and sweating like a stripper in church, so it was quite the challenge to see anything clearly. It just so happened, that Austin's vantage point in the room positioned Melissa in his contorted line of vision through said mirror. The pain that raced through his inner thigh and groin muscles released a shit load of endorphins, making it feel like he copped a bag of dope before class. While his body straddled the thin line between pleasure and pain, his eyes saw legs, ass and beaver outlines and then sent that information to his brain, which responded by pumping blood to his penis.

So, as he lay stretched on his blue Yoga mat and completely counter to all of his efforts to stay low-key, Austin was suddenly in possession of a world-class boner. He cringed at the thought of a woman in the class looking over at the bulge in his sweatpants, so he thought about the cast of "The Golden Girls" and the brace face girl on "Ugly Betty" and thought of them all in the buff. That, combined with painful thoughts of having multiple root canals without anesthesia and his jousting Johnson was subdued.

When the Yoga instructor mercifully ended the class, Austin looked around the room as the women began to socialize a bit, and noticed how they all glowed in the aftermath of physical exertion. It was that distinct look a woman had after a sweaty, lengthy sex romp, which was usually followed by either:

1.sleep
2.cuddling
3.cigarettes
4.sportscenter
5.Red wine

He finally got a glimpse of the face that was attached to the body and he initially thought it was a girl that looked like Melissa if she had cut her hair and was sporting a serious South American tan. He was making his way over to the Yoga instructor for a quick chat, while trying to keep his male presence as unobtrusive as possible. Austin thought, perhaps, that his presence would make some of the women uncomfortable, which, in turn, would make him feel uncomfortable and with that feeling ultimately turning to anger over the ladies making him feel weird.

Austin stumbled a bit with his introduction to the instructor and the sudden burst of baritone voice directed attention to his presence in the room. He could feel some of the other class members looking him over a bit, so Austin figured that the girl who resembled Melissa was doing the same. The acoustics in the room made Austin's conversation with the instructor quite audible over the din of group chatter.

He said something about the lotus position and eastern culture just so the instructor thought that he was really into it and not at the class for the broads, which he wasn't. Austin directed the conversation around to an absurd topic to see if the girl with the lovely beaver outline was Melissa.

Instructor
"Everyone should practice the art of Yoga"
Austin
"I agree-it centers you and that betters your life"
Instructor
"I've been concentrating on Wall Street workers because they would benefit from Yoga"
Austin
"I agree-even ZOO KEEPERS would benefit from taking Yoga"
Instructor
"Uh, yeah even zookeepers"
Austin
"Puts you in harmony with the animals and all"
Instructor
"That's right, that's so true"
Austin
"I have a friend whose father is a ZOO KEEPER-I'll ask her to bring him to your class"
Instructor
"This is OUR class"

Austin
"You're right-bring him to our class"

Austin said it and then looked in the direction of the girl whom he thought to be Melissa. He craned his neck a bit for a better view and there it was, the delicate ballerinas were dancing in her eyes and her smile was holding back laughter as she spoke to another member of the class. After a few more awkward moments with the yoga instructor, who was quite the looker herself, Austin excused himself to towel off and walked towards Melissa. She was looking directly at him, smiling like a Cheshire cat as the other classmate excused herself to go change.

Nathan began speaking to her like they just saw each other yesterday and the conversation fell in line from there.

Austin
"You've got quite a stretch"
Melissa
"Not really, I'm just getting it back"
Austin
"Damn, can't tell"
Melissa
"Thank you, I think"
Austin
"I didn't know you take this class?"
Melissa
"It's my first time here actually"
Austin
"I'm starving"
Melissa
"I'm sweaty"
Austin
"You want to get some food after you shower?"
Melissa
"I feel sticky and nasty"

Austin
"Is that a no?"
Melissa
"It's food at my place"
Austin
"What am I easy?"
Melissa
"I was hoping you were still hard"
Austin
"Wait, how did you see that?"

Austin found out lots of stuff that night, one of which was he didn't like when a girl tries to pop her finger up his arse during sex. He also found out that Melissa's relationship with Dillon had expired and, after they broke up, she went to Argentina to clear her head. Melissa stayed with a really good friend and the girl's family for three months and was tempted to relocate down there permanently. She was also into a holistic lifestyle now and spoke of the wonders that a good colon cleansing would do for overall body health and how yoga grounded her soul.

Austin listened intently as Melissa delved into her feelings and made pronouncements of a newfound awareness, a new connection with the world and how she purged the bad elements from her life. He also dozed off a few times while she was talking from the kitchen and may have missed a few other things while she was taking a shower (she left the bathroom door open so she could talk!) but overall he gathered that Melissa was very happy and enjoyed a rejuvenated passion for life.

Though Austin was very pleased that Melissa was genuinely happy, subconsciously, he wished that she wasn't so centered. It's crazy, but Austin was afraid that he was the essence of the bad elements that Melissa had recently purged from her life. He was pretty fucked up in the head at that point in time. Hell, he had been fucked up in the head for quite a while and would have probably enjoyed a girl that was equally as fucked.

Austin and Melissa began seeing each other from that moment at the yoga class, yet Austin figured it was only a matter of time before Melissa saw him for what he really was and let him go. Looking back, he clearly saw how he acted upon those subconscious fears, which activated his dirty self-sabotage mechanism and spoiled their relationship.

The self-sabotage mechanism manifested by Austin being dodgy, removed, and sporting a world-class wandering eye. He would use the art of subtle deception to steal looks at chicks at every occasion. He would even enlist Melissa in his efforts by pointing out random hot girls and commenting on their jeans or haircut. In retrospect, Austin wasn't really being very subtle; he was as obvious as an ink spot on a white oxford shirt. He felt that his relationship with Melissa was counting down to termination, and, like the final seconds of a Knicks blowout loss at The Garden, it was hard to watch.

Austin felt that several of the events which eventually sealed his fate with Melissa, weren't his fault at all. One in particular was a total set-up. Jenny, a psycho friend of Melissa's, really had it in for Austin. She thought that Melissa and her ex-boyfriend Dillon should be back together, mainly for the perks Jenny enjoyed from that relationship; trips to L.A. and Paris, dinner at Nobu and constant partying at clubs. Since Melissa found Dillon to be quite boring when they were alone, she insisted that Jenny tag along to many of their social and recreational engagements.

According to Jenny, her swag bag of fun dried up when Austin popped up into Melissa's life. It's not like Austin stole Melissa from Dillon or caused dissension in their relationship by whispering sweet nothings in her ear. In fact, he hadn't seen her for several months after Melissa and Dillon broke up. Melissa really liked Austin and Jenny was determined to put an end to it, simply because Austin couldn't fly them off to Paris and stay at the 5 Rue de Moussy hotel like Dillon could and would do.

In the past, he'd been guilty of not accepting responsibility for his actions but this wasn't one of those situations. Jenny truly set Austin up and the decisive event began quite innocently. Austin was sent a text message, from a text message user group, which invited him to Marquee for a friend's surprise birthday party. It was in the upstairs room on Saturday night and started at eleven thirty. It should be noted that Austin usually reserved his nightlife activities to the weekdays because the weekend brought out all of the nut jobs.

The nut jobs spilled pomegranate martinis all over the place and pestered the DJ with requests for Lindsey Lohan remixes. People were drunk on the weekdays as well, but on Saturday night, the nutty girls were usually accompanied by juiced up boyfriends, fresh out of Gold's gym. The types of dudes that acted like they owned the whole club and would inevitably wind up in a fight by the end of the night. They pushed and shoved and never, ever apologized for stepping all over people as they made their way to the bar. Those things, combined with the tragically low fashion IQ of weekend club goers made them a terror to be around.

Anyway, Austin showed up at Marquee with his friend Ryan, who was the perfect weekend party pal. Ryan had way too much energy and was guaranteed to keep a laugh going throughout the night, even though the music sucked, the drinks were light and your kicks were getting ruined. Austin got upstairs and started looking for his friend. It immediately dawned on Austin that Marquee was not the type of club where his friend Carla would have a surprise birthday party and he actually didn't remember it being her birthday.

He didn't call her to double check because it was supposed to be a surprise and since he got the text the day of the party, he didn't have a chance to verify with other friends if it was her birthday. Just as he thought that he should find Ryan, who had already wandered off or call Carla to see if it was her birthday party, an incredibly hot and slutty girl approached him.

She was wearing a slouchy red dress that was incredibly sexy, clung to her hips and hung open to reveal her décolleté. In perfect accompaniment, she wore a pair of weathered rock and roll cowboy boots that looked like they stayed on during sex. So out of the blue, she came up and asked Austin to do a shot of Jameson's with her while she waited for her friends. She gave the offer such a sexy yet slutty delivery that it sounded like a line from a porno movie!

A man that turned down a shot of whiskey from a girl like that is…well he probably didn't get dumped by a great girl like Melissa. But what did he know, Austin voted for Ralph Nader one year (though it was on a drunken bet while out on a date). So off to the bar they went as she grabbed Austin's hand and led him through the crowd. Now any guy in his right mind knows that if you met that type of girl in a big club, on a weekend and she asked you to do a shot of whiskey with her as she took your hand; she wasn't going to Sunday service in the morning.

If the thirty minutes that followed was filmed in a time sequence, it would have started with Austin at the bar downing his first shot

-Then he's downing his second shot right after and feeling a little hot
-Then his third shot as security pulls the girl down from dancing on the bar
-Then he's downstairs in the big room at Marquee acting like Patrick Swayze
-Then he had his shirt off and the girl in the red dress was down his pants
-Then the slutty girl's friends arrive and Austin's a meat sandwich, to the chagrin of every guy and three-drink lesbian within 25 feet
-Then Austin was flicking the pierced tongue of the red dress girl

-THEN HE'S DANCING RIGHT NEXT TO MELISSA AND
HER FRIEND JENNY WHO WERE BOTH LOOKING
RIGHT AT HIM
-THEN THE GIRLS THAT AUSTIN WERE DANCING
WITH WERE SMILING AT HIM LIKE HE WAS THE
BIGGEST SUCKER IN THE WORLD
-THEN...............

Austin never found out how much debauchery
Melissa actually bore witness to, though he asked a few
times in an attempt to gauge the depth of the shit that he
was in. In retrospect, the whole situation was such an
obvious set up. Jenny orchestrated the whole thing and
brought Melissa there to drive a wedge through Austin's
relationship with Melissa and it totally worked, because it
was shortly afterwards that the Melissa/Austin thing
ended.
Maybe "ended" didn't properly frame what
happened; perhaps "changed" was more fitting. Austin
tried talking about it to Melissa, yet she never tried to listen.
It wasn't an ugly break-up. In fact, it was more of a steady
but gradual separation of their lives. And in about three
weeks it was officially different.

It wasn't like they had announced to each other, at
any point, that they were boyfriend and girlfriend in the
beginning, so they never really had a break-up
conversation. He couldn't say that they retained a
friendship since they were no longer speaking, but Austin
still considered Melissa his friend and he hoped that she
did the same.

CHAPTER 3

His life went from happy to crappy, and Austin was face to face with the void that his time with Melissa filled. He was an architect who had done mainly strip malls and retail installations and he actually hadn't had much work in the last nine months. He had some money in a CD, five hundred stocks of Apple Computer and a savings account, but was petrified that he'd end up destitute; yet he wasn't hustling to find work. He allowed his relationship with Melissa to take up lots of his time on purpose, since he was avoiding the reality that he really needed a job.

If he were a wee better looking with washboard abs he could become a gigolo, fleecing older broads of their holdings. He would actually need to get a better wardrobe, a haircut, stop grabbing his nuts in public and would probably do well to learn another language, since any self-respecting gigolo was fluent in at least one of the Latin based languages.

After all the time spent without a job or even a prospect for a job over the last nine months he was finally on the cusp of something really good, a project that he developed and that someone was interested in and here he was, fucking it up. On the train, running late for an important meeting was not where Austin was supposed to be at that moment.

When folks on the subway shifted their position, Austin's line of vision to the other side of the train cleared and he was relieved to see that the guy wasn't one of the Dillons. With nothing to read, Austin was left looking at train advertisements for the entire ride. The 1-800-lawyer ads guaranteed money for slip and falls, automobile accidents or medical malpractice. Those ads were some of his personal favorites on the subway.

Austin always thought that it was a certain type of law firm that advertised on the NYC subway. It was the ambulance chasing, sly as a hooker with rent due type of lawyer and yet they were making money hand over foot. But why not, he thought to himself, who doesn't need a lawyer? Drug pushers, Senators, celebrities and corporate CEOs all need a lawyer. Hell, even lawyers need lawyers in the litigious society that is America, where kids sue their parents for emancipation. If you can't afford a lawyer…well then you take your butt on "Judge Judy" and air your dirty laundry on the tube.

Austin joked to himself, only to take his mind off of his plight. He snuck a peak at nine to five working women and admired their ankles. They were strong, ready for the world, while he felt totally opposite. The hot chic across and down was listening to her iPod, bobbing her head with reckless abandon. The girl next to her was doing the same thing, rocking out and mouthing the words to The Stones "Satisfaction".

Austin was trying diligently to forget that he was running late, again, and how un-fresh that was. He knew the whole thing. Like a soothsayer, he knew exactly how it was going to pan out. Perhaps he was channeling Ms. Cleo, the shamed television psychic. She didn't actually have psychic ability according to the class action suit brought against the Psychic Network, but then again neither did Austin; he simply had a sickening case of déjà vu. He knew how the situation was going to turn out because he lived it before.

It's fear of success that had placed Austin in such a familiar situation. He thought that it was a self-sabotage mechanism which was subconsciously activated whenever something good was about to happen. He triggered it himself, yet always felt very cliché about it. He felt it was psychological mumbo jumbo if he knew that he was doing something negative to himself, yet didn't pump the brakes and put an end to it.

Austin realized that he didn't have the exact address to the place memorized and after looking through his bag, he realized that he didn't bring the little, itsy bitsy piece of paper on which he jotted it down. Luckily, Austin knew the name of the company that he was visiting and also the street that it was located on, which was good. It was better than having no information at all he thought.

That was a lie actually, because it really sucked. Austin's lack of an address would have been a small hiccup in the plan if he was running early and a real inconvenience if he was running right on time; but since he was running behind nearly twenty minutes it was a disaster. That thought was barreling through Austin's head like a pinball bumping synapses when he noticed, through the scratchetti scarred train windows, that the train was barreling past 23rd street. 23rd street, his stop. Austin glanced over at the window with the train line designation and was smirked at by a big ole' A.

It felt like the A laughed and whispered Austin's ineptness into the ear of each and every passenger on the train. Like the A train leaked his shit life into the shiny white iPods of the masses and told of his failures and self-betrayal. He felt that the A train told riders of the failures that drove him crazy and mocked him. Mocked him viciously and called him a loser. What he really needed was the C train making local stops, yet Austin was on the A express train barreling towards failure.

Austin was no longer going to make the meeting. He was no longer going to present his brilliant proposal, which was many weeks in the making. He felt that he wasn't moving forward in his life. Not just standing still, which was bad, but he felt that he was actually moving in reverse. He felt like he was falling. He was working against the clock and the clock was working against him.

He was no longer thinking of the "oh so believable" reason of why he was running late to that "oh so important" meeting. He'd moved on to a bigger, more complete and utterly enveloping failure. He's stepped up, or stepped down in fact, to the big story about why he couldn't make the meeting. Not a day before the meeting or an hour before the meeting but twenty-five minutes past the start of a potentially incredible opportunity.

Perhaps he should walk in front of a slow moving vehicle and add a dramatic flair to the poor excuse for letting himself down, Austin thought. He should pick an expensive, yet leisurely paced sports car to instigate his explanation, his reason for not calling and wasting people's time.

This "accident" had to have happened en route to the meeting, which was why he didn't call. This type of thinking normally remains a thought, yet suddenly the answer for Austin was clear as day. It was the only logical answer. The only salve for a festering, open wound that was his life was sudden contact with a car.

He couldn't think about it, he had to just do it. Like the Nike motto, it wouldn't be easy but the difficulty of the task didn't matter. In fact that task couldn't be easy. It had to challenge the very survival instinct that surges within every human being. It must be total commitment and follow through. It was a test that Austin felt he must pass. He was always quite exceptional at standardized tests, which was how he was going to attack the challenge.

He actually needed to enlist an unwitting friend to be an audio witness to the impending accident. Someone that could tell the world that he'd been hit and how it happened. Austin scrolled through the numbers in his phone yet couldn't make a conscious decision on which poor sap it would be. Whomever he called was being brought into something that was one big lie to cover up complete slackness, yet if it went wrong then it's a death and who wants to be an ear witness to a murder, especially when it's burning their Anytime minutes!

He randomly punched letters into his phone and was going to accept the name that was brought up, but unfortunately the name that popped up was totally the wrong person. In fact he should have removed that girls name from his cell phone. If he called her and duped her into witnessing the event, Austin knew that she would surely root for the car to hit him, back up and hit him again. He cleared the search, punched in some more random letters and came up with his mom.

The next try yielded pay dirt-a person of shady ethics, questionable morals and a fine imagination. It was Carla whose college roommate was the person Austin was supposed to have met about his project. She wouldn't even catch on until later at the hospital and by then he would have created a wonderful excuse for not making the meeting and Carla could relay his unfortunate accident to all relevant parties. Besides, it was on the pretense of her birthday party that he was lured to Marquee the night he was set up by Melissa's friend Jenny, so Austin felt like Carla owned him in a sense. Not that the thought *made* any sense, but he was no longer a sensible person.

Hell, he might even catch some airtime on the local 6 o'clock news if it's a slow news day, Austin thought to himself. Hopefully there wouldn't be a Bush administration embarrassment or major wall-street malfeasance dominating the twenty-two minutes of actual TV time that was available to tell the story. Austin stood on the corner of 34th street and 7th avenue and surveyed the scene. The traffic was stifling. The sidewalks teemed with people pressing against one another. Jostling, pushing, maneuvering, and cussing at the crush, rushing ahead of the people in the front only to find themselves behind even more people.

The pedestrian jam meant the cars had no choice but to move slowly. Mr. Potential Accident scanned the street for the right car to get his whole thing going yet couldn't find the correct vehicle. There was a string of new SUV's rolling around, controlling the streets like Shaq under the basket. The Escalades and Expeditions were boss over the smattering of compacts and sedans, along with the ford Taurus' K Cars and other official government business vehicles.

None of those particular cars were ideal for the job, yet that brilliant deduction in the moment meant nothing; because Austin really needed to get hit by the right car ASAP and time was running out fast. Without a viable vehicle to instigate his disgusting excuse, Austin quickly decided to hop in a cab and head to Soho to stage his accident. He figured a location change would do the trick.

The ride from Herald Square to Soho was filled with anxiety. Austin didn't ponder his actions too deeply since he was resigned to the need for the outcome and spent the ensuing minutes calculating if his fine production would be timely enough to work. He couldn't stage an accident an hour after the meeting time. He knew that the accident needed to be within striking distance to the start time of the meeting that he bungled. If it weren't timely, then it would backfire and appear that he simply blew everybody off.

Austin thought about the outcome of this accident in its many potential manifestations, but thought long and hard about the one definite outcome of the accident-getting hurt; and specifically about getting hurt without any health insurance to pay his medical bills. It was a prime reason that he needed to get whacked by a luxury sports car. There was no way around pain and more to the point; pain was a necessary outcome if the whole thing was to be successful. If it's a Toyota Corolla, then the odds of the person having some car insurance, let alone some personal wealth, was diminished substantially.

Austin may have a story, an excuse for his absence from the meeting and perhaps a spot on the local evening news after the accident, but he would still be jobless, running out of money and possibly paralyzed from the waist down. As he looked out the window of the taxi, he thought that a paraplegic with a lively mind had to be living in a personal prison. Austin didn't like any type of imprisonment, Sing Sing or otherwise, and hoped that whoever hit him was not among the reported fifteen percent of uninsured drivers on the road.

The cab made its way down Broadway and passed NYU as scores of college kids stood around between classes, smoking cigarettes, laughing and scarfing down supersized value meals from the McDonalds across the road. Austin wondered if any of those kids realized that they were currently in the best years of their lives. If they realized that the potential of what they could be could run out. That unfulfilled potential could metastasize into toxic poison, turn to paste and glue their eyes shut every morning.

Lost potential is never a thought in college, since potential is frozen by matriculation. That's when a person is "full of potential" and his or her possibilities are endless. Potential starts ticking away upon entrance to the real world and could be lost at various points on the road of life. Lost potential could often be found in the bottom of something that's brown and served in a shot glass. Not dropped there by mistake, like a pendant that slipped off a Gucci link chain but placed there intentionally to lift the burden of a formidable weight.

Like a baby from a teenage mother that was fathered by an uncle, lost potential is often abandoned and frequently found in a bar by Jack or Jameson or Jim Beam. Unlike an in-bred, Ricki Lake sort of baby, lost potential can't be seen or touched or smelled, but it's there nonetheless. It doesn't cast a true reflection, instead reflecting what it has made of the person that it left.

Right around Broadway and Bond Street the cab ran into a small traffic jam. Austin never, ever remembered snarled traffic at that location on Broadway. In perfect pitch with the melody of his life, he was running late to staging his accident. Austin rolled down both back windows and asked the cab driver if it would be cool to smoke a cigarette. They made eye contact through the rear view mirror and the cabbie gave Austin a slight nod of the head, though Austin was already lighting one up.

He pushed the cigarette smoke out through his nose and then through his mouth while aiming it out the window. He became very aware of the heat from the smoke as if it was his first cigarette, like years of smoking had not desensitized the hair in his nostrils and every nerve ending in his mouth.

The whole moment was very slow, which gave Austin a cold tingle. It felt like the slow moments right before your ticket gets punched, Austin thought to himself. Was this the infamous "last cigarette" that always gets requested by the condemned man as he is standing in front of a firing squad? Was he experiencing his "final moments"?

Austin's life suddenly flashed in front of his eyes and to be honest, he didn't think it was so cool. He thought that it was over-hyped like reality television. Like a bad movie that you stayed to see, just so the chic that dragged you there didn't find out what kind of a crazy asshole you were until after you gave her a Dirty Sanchez. You see, this was his third near-death experience. It was truly amazing the first and second times. But by the third time, Austin thought that it really sucked. The third time that his life flashed in front of his eyes, Austin felt that there was a serious dearth of romanticism.

It became simply what it was; a reminder that, in case he forgot, he could be about to die. The first instance occurred when Austin was traveling for business. He crash-landed in Atlanta on a flight from NYC to Houston, though luckily, the plane didn't fall out of the sky and everyone survived. Short of a few bumps and bruises suffered during the landing, the whole ordeal ended up being one huge false alarm. Nonetheless most people thought it was a wrap and were asking God for favors.

Some were probably asking for favors and forgiveness real early, certainly earlier than Austin. The moment the Captain came over the P.A. and told everyone to prepare for a crash landing, those with the largest load to be forgiven started praying, those with a small load thought about it and the Vegan/Health-Nut/Non-smoker/Gym-Member/alternative fuel car driving passenger started cursing his luck; or lack thereof.

Safety being what it is, if an airplane was about to crash to the ground, the captain should tell everyone that they're free to do something pleasurable. It's worse than giving a kid homework over the summer vacation. It's unfair that a person's last moments would be spent in the crash landing position. The position was like doing yoga, and who needs to stretch if you're about to kick the bucket in a few minutes.

If the airplane was going to fall from the sky, the captain should announce that everyone was free to masturbate. A guy wants to squeeze a tit or run to the john or at least smack the noisy kid with the big feet that kept kicking his seat. Tucking your head between your legs was not high on the list of things to do at that moment, like anyone really wants to smell their ass right before they die!

The second life flash was less like a movie, and more like a short film from that TV show Kids In The Hall, as it happened while Austin nearly drowned in a swimming pool at his friend's house in the Hamptons. When swimming was being taught at summer camp, Austin was one of the kids experimenting with pot and on that summer day in the Hamptons, his inability to swim finally came back to haunt him. He actually felt quite stupid as he was drowning in his friend's pool.

There were perhaps forty people at the house, and around thirty of those people Austin knew and really liked. The only thing that Austin kept thinking, as he was gasping for air, was that drowning would be such a bummer, a total downer for the weekend! There's nothing like the accidental death of a friend to douse the fire of fun. But death was not due on that day because at the last minute, a spark of energy and wherewithal emerged and vaulted Austin to the edge of the pool. The spark was borne from the shock and shame that would be felt by his parental units when the police found the copious amounts of recreational drugs amongst his belongings.

What if he was labeled a dealer at his death, without being able to defend himself and his families honor? It would be the worst gift to leave your loved ones before you die, since they would have to deal with the whispers and not have you around to dispel them. That particular fear was the spark that propelled Austin into action. It gave him the spirit to fight and claw, pull on people's legs until he reached the safety of the edge of the pool. It was probably only 4 full feet of frantic swimming, but to Austin it felt like a mile.

Coming close to death was quite traumatic and Austin felt as if he was on his way to yet another episode, but the difference was that he was actively instigating the moment. He was running a few minutes behind in performing a last ditch effort at evading the answers to why he always got the short end of the stick. He was really dodging the reasons why his life was in such shambles. A desperate man often acts in haste and make no bones about it; he was a desperate man.

It's a very peculiar frame of mind that connects blowing a meeting to an intense desire to get hit by a car. It was a frame of mind that Austin didn't know he could attain. He never considered himself to be a desperate person, even in times of great despair. He weathered quite a few personal storms previously without losing his grip on sanity, and without opting for a death-defying act as a way to salvage a situation.

For instance, Austin was homeless for about three days at one juncture; which was something that he rarely spoke about. He had lost his business, lost his apartment, and any semblance of dignity. He moved into his then girlfriend's mother's house because he didn't have a pot to piss in. He lived in that apartment with his girlfriend, her sister and her mother. Austin was completely good for nothing and laid around their house like they owed him something. He damn near ate 'em out of house and home when he wasn't hogging the big TV or smoking pot in the hallway.

Austin didn't contribute to any household expenses, although he was, by far, the biggest expense in the household. After a few months of this obscene behavior, he had completely worn out his welcome. Said girlfriend and he were no longer a couple, so at that point, he was really bumming a place to live. He was the "guy on the couch" from Dave Chappelle's hilarious movie Half-Baked! He couldn't recall the straw that broke the camel's back but he was given two days to pack his shit and hit the road (Jack and don't you come back no more, no more, no more, no more).

He had nowhere to turn. Going to his mother's house was out of the question, since he felt like such a fucking burden. If he turned up on her porch, she would cook him a hot meal and open the door to his old bedroom, but he felt guilty about the very idea. His father's house was also out of the question, since he would look at Austin like he lost his mind and hand him the classified section with some stern advice. Not to mention that Austin's father had remarried and moved to Seattle and Austin had no plans to relocate to such a dreary city.

Austin walked out of that three-bedroom apartment and felt the collective sigh from his ex-girlfriend's whole family as the doorknob hit him where the dog should have bit him. He called up his friend Neil and crashed on his couch for a night before Neil's girlfriend huffed and puffed and blew the couch down. Austin left the next day under the guise of finding a cheap hotel until he sorted himself out but quickly decided that he didn't want to spend the last bit of money he had on some fleabag hotel for a few weeks.

Before you could say, "brother can you spare a quarter" Austin was resting his head in a small park in Greenwich Village and ruing the moment he bolted the three-bedroom apartment with the soft pillows and full refrigerator. He slept in close proximity to a few gentlemen that were down on their luck and who reeked of something cheap and cherry flavored. The same dudes that Austin used to pity were now his neighbors.

Austin felt quite vulnerable and couldn't find a comfortable position in which to drift off and dream of a better life. He had on a shiny, cheap watch that, to someone living on the street, could represent a few days worth of food or a few hits of their favorite demon. He also had one hundred and ninety-two dollars in his pocket, which Austin thought made him, by far, the wealthiest guy laying on the benches.

At some point he fell asleep for some unknown amount of time, because he woke up to the sound of children's laughter. Austin immediately looked around to see if he knew anyone in the park who might be looking at him with a mix of pity and disdain. He saw a gumbo of kids and mothers, some nannies and a few fathers. Austin stood up, dusted himself off, checked his cell phone, which now sported a dead battery, and slinked away with his pride between his legs. He stopped to get a coffee at the deli and re-evaluate his life.

If ever there was a moment for Austin to want to jump in front of a moving car that was it. He was nearly penniless, homeless and even worse, his breath smelled like boiled shit. In retrospect, he guessed the situation was enough to put a fire under his ass, because he pulled it together, found a cheap apartment and made another plan for his life. This was possible, he guessed because he felt like his "potential" was still percolating. He was able to look past the situation at hand to envision a better life. It was the potential, or lack thereof, that made Austin so desperate as he rode in the cab down Broadway.

Austin was having depressing thoughts of being washed up, homeless and middle aged in NYC and it made him cringe. He would rather be dead, he thought. He walked past a homeless couple the other day. They were lying on the sidewalk, asleep in a tender embrace. He imagined the youth of those two people brimming with possibilities. He wondered about the route that landed them on the ground in front of a library in the east village.

Austin's three-day homeless stint seared a resolve into his mind that would propel him into a self-sacrificial, life ending movement if he ever felt that his potential had expired. With that mindset, it was clear that the decision to jump in front of a moving car (and all that it entailed) was on autopilot. It was almost like a self-destruct button that gets triggered automatically. Austin thought that he'd surely run outta potential, and that his possibilities were no longer endless. In fact, he felt that his possibilities had abruptly ended at the exact moment that the A train whistled past Twenty Third Street.

He thought to hop out of the cab at Bond Street and run to Soho but quickly vetoed the action. Instead Austin dialed up Carla's phone to begin the "witness to an accident" phase of that shitty, pitiful drama. Perhaps, if he wanted a positive outcome to the charade, he needed to utilize positive thinking. This was actually a superb production of a modern tragedy, like an updated Shakespeare piece and he really needed to nail the character. At Houston Street, Carla's phone rang…and rang and rang and rang. He tried again and it rang out to voicemail. Oh shit, the production was becoming unraveled Austin thought.

He got out of the cab, flicked his cigarette, gave the driver twenty dollars and told him to keep the change. But Austin asked for the receipt and the other receipts that were dangling out of the meter. Since the receipts had times on them he could use a receipt that was time-stamped a half hour earlier, to show that he was heading to the meeting but hopped out to get something in Soho when *bam*, he was smacked up by some pretentious prick in a fancy fucking sports car. You know *those* types of cars with *those* types of drivers abound in Soho, which made the story even more plausible.

Austin's original plan was to head over to the Soho Grand where he could stage his demented melodrama for the trendy guests at the hotel, but since time was of the essence, the Apple store on Prince Street would have to suffice. The area was packed with people and a procession of lithe European driving machines that crept past the corner of Prince and Greene Street. The problem was that they were moving so slow that the impact from a hit wouldn't hurt a brittle boned grandma with a walker.

Suddenly, five cars from the Escalade at the corner he spotted a red roadster, driven by an irate and impatient driver. He looked determined to get to downtown Cipriani for lunch with his hot little mistress. The guy looked a little stressed out actually and didn't look like he was having a good day. He leaned on his horn with insolence but still caught the red light two cars back from the corner, letting out a string of invectives and pounding his steering wheel with both fists.

It was thirty seconds, or whatever the time it took for a light to turn from red to green, until the tragedy unfolded. Austin stood on the corner and searched his pockets for some misplaced key or lost credit card in an effort to calm his nerves. He kept thinking that in a few seconds, the agitated asshole wreathing with anxiety in Corinthian leather seats would smash the gas pedal and green light the production. The next fifteen seconds were in slow motion. The accident needed to look spontaneous and in the moment, so he cleared his mind of everything except the lone task of getting hit by that car.

Austin felt like a Hollywood stunt man about to earn his keep. At ten seconds 'til his close-up, his phone vibrated. He glanced at the screen and saw Carla's name and number flash as a missed call and also saw the voicemail symbol flashing at the top right corner. He instinctively hit the voicemail button, even though he should have been preparing for the accident and focusing on the matter at hand.

Austin had the cell phone to his ear when he suddenly heard his name called out. He turned his head for a moment but then turned right back around to face the traffic. In a flush of self-consciousness, he felt foolish and outted about the jackass stunt he was about to attempt. At three seconds, he heard asshole's engine throttle. At two seconds, Austin made a motion to cross, hesitated to let the two cars pass and with the precision of an N.A.T.O. strike, he lunged into the street.

In the three seconds it took to go through the intersection, the Porsche picked up considerable momentum. It gained more speed than Austin anticipated and though under the speed limit, it was going just fast enough to change the outcome of his insane, selfish and presumptuous one-man act.

Austin spent the half of second before impact locking eyes with the driver of the car and he noticed that his face looked freaked out. Horror, shock and disappointment in his whole life oscillated freely around Austin's physical form and then it was black.

CHAPTER 4

It was the lack of a loving relationship that strayed Nathan's heart in search of fulfillment outside of his marriage; or that was the lone justification that he soothed himself with in those rare moments of guilt. Though he was never the symbol of monogamy, having indulged in a few feverish but frivolous flings with a few females, it was still the first time that he had vested feelings into another woman outside of his wife.

It was strange and altered how he normally dealt with the situation. It didn't matter to Nathan in the long run as it was the nature of men to do such things he always thought. In the same way that chickens bark and a cow meows, Nathan did what was natural. He had never elevated a side chic over the mother of his child until Missy came along. She made him work extra hard to stick to his self-imposed rules of creeping.

If nothing, those moments of infidelity were a re-broadcast of his childhood. It was a made for TV dramatization of his life as a child, when he lived with his father and stepmother. The infidelity continuum bore witness to each of his torrid moments where vows were broken and promises rendered to mere words. Nathan figured that cheating was only such if he got caught and for many years he had been the king of covert carnal hook-ups! But in the same manner that it's questioned whether a fallen tree makes a noise in an empty forest, it begged the question of whether creeping was wrong if no one knew about it.

A tax cheat was only labeled as such when the IRS put the dogs out to recoup that which was constitutionally owed to them and gains a conviction in a court of law. In the same light, a cheater bears that title only when busted and Nathan was too careful for that. Dirty dancing in discos was a no-no. Groping in public was against the rules and the rules were not made to be broken.

It was important to take these precautions because the urge for extra-marital sex was strong but Nathan's fear of a pit-bull divorce lawyer, hired by an angry and scorned wife was stronger. So as it stood, Nathan was a no good, dirty, cheating, sexist, misguided fool, but he was definitely a careful one!

Nathan knew that he needed to do several things while on his extended lunch break. He carefully broke down the drill to his secretary so that she didn't flub her lines. He instructed her, for all intent and purposes, that he was out on meetings and wouldn't be back for a few hours unless it was his wife, in which case he was busy in the office and unavailable. He also gave her instructions to pay his car insurance as he recently got a letter at the office that it lapsed. He quizzed her again to make sure that they were on the same page, switched his blackberry to "office" and headed out the door to grab a large glass of pressed wheat grass and melon juice at his favorite juice bar. On the elevator down, the afternoon played out in his head and put a smile on his face.

It was the type of anticipation that always made his heart palpitate. The anticipation formed as a spinal tingle that would then engorge his entire being with enough energy to light a city block. Such an electric state could birth moments of resounding oneness with the world and clarity of existence, creating an outer body experience. It's like career day in grade school, when the kid that loved animals stumbled upon the zoology table and his entire, budding existence yelled out "Yatzy"!

Nathan was addicted. He was addicted to the wave that wiped him over as he planned for such moments. Planning for *that* moment. The moment that tasted like nothing yet sweeter than anything he'd ever put in his mouth. It was how he came to define his life. It's the cat that he kept chasing and he didn't know why. He did know why but he didn't know WHY! But that's what it was. That's what it was and he couldn't change it or better yet, he was unwilling to consider not chasing it. He wouldn't capitulate to the notion that it was wrong or cow-tow to reasoning, in any fucking form, about why it was wicked for him to chase the cat.

Was that selfish? It's rhetorical because it was, but it didn't matter. Was it self-serving. Again, it was rhetorical. The awareness that he was a slave to feelings spawned by a beautiful, naked woman had not given rise to a rebellion against his deceitful ways; it's actually forced him to accept it as it is.

It forced Jordan to accept himself and live in comfort with his actions. He was past regret. Nathan was past shame and guilt and felt no remorse, so conversely he embraced his infidelity. It wasn't as if Nathan was ever the ideal husband, though it was still with hesitation, doubt and trepidation that he moved through his illicit affairs. But before the cheating and lying, before the fear of divorce lawyers and alimony, there was a set of experiences. Those experiences planted seeds in the soil of his heart and soul, eventually sprouting in his mind and spreading throughout his being like Ivy. Though initially light and spotty, this poisonous ivy soon entangled his feelings and his thinking, eventually strangling his heart and mind with belief in inherent human deceit.

Early on Nathan had a unique relationship with girls. He had a way of making them feel comfortable around him. His first memory of the dynamic that exists between girls and boys was with Vinnie Coleman's little sister. Vinnie Coleman was the best baseball player on the block; that's unless you asked Nathan's brother who was quite the pitcher in his own right. On the other hand, Nathan was into sports but he wasn't into organized sports.

He would play pickup football and baseball or basketball in the schoolyard but wasn't into the whole regimentation thing and definitely wasn't into practice. The whole notion of practice made no sense to Nathan since he never wanted to hone his athletic ability. He liked the beauty of hitting a baseball without teaching, of shaking and outracing a defender in football without a bunch of instruction.

So when all the other little boys were off going to tryouts and practice for some sport, Nathan was at home filling his time in other ways; one of which was feeling up Felicia, Vinnie Coleman's little sister. He was only in the third grade at the time but he was advanced in the feeling in his pants. He knew that the relief to the pressure building up behind his zipper lay between Felicia Coleman's legs. At least he thought that it did and he was off on a fact-finding mission each and every Saturday while the rest of the boys were off playing with a ball.

The main problem with being a third grader and fooling around was that there was never a proper place to do it. As a result, Nathan had to run his little third grade game in every available location. He made moves on Felicia in the vestibule of his house, the coat room at school and ironically, the doghouse in Felicia's backyard. The Coleman family had a huge St. Bernard that usually stayed inside the Coleman house, but for times of banishment due to visitors or housecleaning, they built the dog a house in the back.

Because the dog was huge, the doghouse consequently, was huge and to a third grader it was the ideal place to roll around and perfect the art of dry humping. Besides the dog hair that was all over the place, Nathan had no problem making out in the dog house. In fact, keeping with lowdown tradition, Nathan actually brought Anthony's little sister Brenda into the Coleman doghouse for a round of dry-humping……….a few times.

The difficulty level of convincing a third grade girl to dry-hump in her backyard should be noted, though convincing a third grade girl to hump in the doghouse of her classmate who lived across the street was even more challenging. It was all in a day for Nathan as a kid. It wasn't just the sex, or pursuit of that 1st time, where Nathan was good with the girls. They would often seek him out during recess or ring his bell after school. He would turn rope for the girls if one of their friends was on punishment or play jacks with them on the stoop.

He was also the recipient of countless batches of rookie cookies. Those were the cookies that little girls make when they were first allowed into the kitchen to bake. Either that or the cookies came from one of the Holly Hobby confection ovens that seemed a rite of passage for all the young girls on Nathan's block. The other boys envied Nathan because of that, especially since he would rub it in that he had cookies and they didn't.

The years went on and though Nathan was good with the girls, he was still a virgin at seventeen-years-old. His first girlfriend in High School was the horniest girl alive and was quite upset when he decided he didn't want to have sex with her. Nathan didn't actually make a declaration, but he made it be known that it was going to happen when he wanted it to happen and not because she was a grown woman masquerading in the body of a fifteen-year-old girl. They would go to Nathan's house after school and since his stepmother was a schoolteacher and didn't get home for another forty-five minutes, it was always a make-out session from the moment that they walked in the door.

Her name was Sara and she was super hot to trot. She always wore sexy, frilly mini-skirts and little lace bobby socks with a tube top, which was Nathan's first lesson on "easy access" clothing. Sara had the hairiest crotch ever and after feeling around for several seconds, while making out, Nathan would usually find a handful of gushy, ready teenage love. In the upstairs TV room, with the after-school sun beaming through the window, her mini-skirt and tube top meeting around her waist, Sara would implore Nathan to deliver the package; but alas, the postman skipped her mailbox.

It was that experience with Sara that shaped the nexus of his belief that girls really wanted it as much as boys. It also took the fun out of it. It removed the chase, the fulfillment of conquest, which was an essential part of the act. It suppressed his visceral carnal vision, which only sees sex, and removed him from the moment that they were supposed to be sharing.

Once removed from the moment, Nathan noticed little things about Sara; like one tit was slightly bigger than the other and that she had a few long strands of hair on her nipples. To notice that was like complaining about a small scratch on a Lexus! It really highlighted that Nathan was not into Sara, so he broke up with her before he headed off to camp for the summer.

It was inevitable to him, though it must have come as a huge surprise to Sara as she cried like a newborn baby while Nathan's father pulled the car away from the house. Perhaps he could have told her a few weeks earlier that he was going away for the summer, but he was no fool. Sara had quite the little temper that could pop up if she didn't get what she wanted and he didn't want to sour the end of the school year with a huge fight. Sara probably thought that Nathan would submit during the heat of July and August and that they would eventually engage in some cabin stabbin', but oh was she wrong.

Fortuitously, it was at summer camp that Nathan met Andrea, his second girlfriend, who was the girl to whom he would finally lose his virginity. It wasn't actually summer camp as much as it was an academic program for city kids during the idle summer months. Kids that were a bit slow were put into remedial classes, the advanced kids were put in college level classes and most importantly all kids were put into college dormitories without parental guidance for six weeks.

The only thing standing between sex, drugs and rock and roll were the horror flick clichéd counselors. They were horny, late teenagers or early twenty somethings who were often so distracted with their own lives that they didn't notice the wanton behavior all around them. That was one of the positives of the program. In fact, most of the kids spent most of their energy trying to hook up.

Andrea was a pretty girl whose family was originally from North Carolina and though she didn't have a southern accent, she did retain a bit of country twang in her voice. She was a year younger than Nathan but looked like a woman. She had a teenage body that was then vogue to blame on hormones in the dairy products.

Nathan first saw Andrea during orientation as the kids were meeting each other and getting introduced to the counselors. He met a bunch of really cute girls that day including Anna, Mandy, Fiona, Candice, Veronica and Jackie, not to mention a few of the female counselors who were also pretty hot. Nathan liked so many girls initially that he would spend his free time daydreaming about them being naked.

The summer wore on, attraction happened and the natural filtering process occurred, and though Nathan liked a few other girls, he was really fond of Andrea. He spent the good part of the summer program pursuing her or rather, trying to get laid, while she spent a good part of it fending him off. They would often go into the unoccupied dormitories and make out for hours, while Nathan's dick got hard as times in 1929. Andrea pronounced early on, that it would be at least three months until she would even consider having sex with Nathan, which Nathan simply considered a challenge. She liked him and all, but she wasn't ready to give it up yet she said.

Nathan and Andrea spent the summer program getting to know each other and by the end of the six-weeks, they were boyfriend and girlfriend. Unfortunately, though not for a lack of effort, Nathan went home from the program with his virginity still intact. Once back home and nearly inseparable in a hot and stifling city apartment, the ability of Andrea to keep Nathan out of her panties waned considerably. Right before the summer break was over, Nathan lost his virginity to Andrea and before long they were fucking like bunnies heading into the new school year.

Each day after the final bell at his school, Nathan would high tail it over to Andrea's high school to pick her up. Though she attended a Catholic school and got out a half-hour earlier than Nathan, Andrea would still wait for him to walk her home. They would walk straight up Lincoln Boulevard, turn left on Pour Avenue and head down the Hill, all while Nathan was catching wood from the sights bestowed by the breeze blowing up Andrea's short, pleated uniform skirt. They would make a right on Brown Street to her building, past the two front doors and onto the elevator to the third floor.

Once inside the apartment it was never ending sex. Nathan and Andrea had six hours of unsupervised time before Andrea's mother returned home from her job in lower Manhattan. That meant sex, sex, sex, which lead to even more sex. After her mother came home from work, made some food, smoked a joint and collapsed from exhaustion in her bed, Andrea and Nathan would sneak off to the kitchen or to the bathroom for more humping. In a few months, Nathan went from being a virgin to having sex three times a day to being pussy whipped with his nose wide open.

Needless to say, he was really feeling Andrea. Fast-forward to his magnificent senior prom, which actually was the crowning moment to a wonderful year; yet it actually commenced the season of his discontent. After graduating from high school, Nathan didn't go away to the summer program with Andrea.

He was headed to Springfield College in the fall and decided to take summer classes there instead. His career counselor suggested it as a good way to get a jump on the school year. He could make friends and start relationships, which was especially important since he would be commuting for the first year.

He wouldn't get a chance to bond with his classmates over lunch in the cafeteria or by lounging in the dorm, so he should "get in where he fit in" which was over the summer. Nathan also figured it would be beneficial academically if he copped a few credits before the first semester began. He saw the upside to getting ahead of the game for once. Sadly, it was all downhill with Nathan and Andrea from that point on. The decline was only noticeable in retrospect since life went on with no visible glitches for at least another year.

It was after his freshman year in college, after going to Andrea's prom and attending her high school graduation that something peculiar happened. Andrea's mom threw a small graduation party for her only daughter at their apartment and amongst Andrea's friends was a dude name Ed. Ed was at the summer program with Andrea the past summer. It was the summer that Nathan opted to go to the freshman orientation at Springfield College, when Ed and Andrea became friends.

Nathan thought that Andrea and Ed were acting a little strange at the party, though he couldn't put his finger on exactly what it was. Andrea was killing it with her tight creme sweater and creme leather skirt with the slit up the side, though Nathan couldn't tell who was showing more admiration towards Andrea, him or Ed. It almost felt like she had two boyfriends at her graduation party.

At the end of the night, Nathan casually questioned Andrea about what happened at the summer program when he wasn't there. He asked her which counselors returned, if they had any cool parties and also asked who was hooking up at the program. He was dancing around the question of whether she cheated on him the previous summer but that was where his line of questioning was leading.

He never asked before, partially because he trusted her and also because he felt that jealousy was ugly, but at that moment he started to regret that decision. If she did cheat, it was so long ago that she could lie about it without effort or a trace of guilt on her face or in her voice. After several minutes the subject was dropped before it got really heated, especially since Nathan didn't have any real grounds to make accusations.

Andrea applied for, and was accepted to several colleges and chose Putnam College, right outside of Atlantic City in Southern New Jersey. She was excited to be going to school and spoke with anticipation in her voice whenever the subject came up. Nathan saw Andrea a few times after her graduation and before she went to Putnam for summer classes and orientation, yet it was during that time that Andrea came clean on her feelings about Nathan and how she planned on dealing with their relationship.

Andrea often complained that Nathan didn't bring her up to Springfield College for his entire freshman year and she was right, but for good reason. Nathan was a commuter, and at any school in America, the commuter was a second-class student. Commuters didn't enjoy the full college experience. Nathan couldn't bring her up to school. Why, how? He didn't have a dorm room or an off-campus apartment.

He didn't have a car and he didn't live close to school. Nathan went to some of the college parties without Andrea, but it was kind of awkward to bring her along. He caught a ride with friends and didn't want to burden them with picking up and dropping her off. Besides, she went to parties without Nathan and it wasn't a problem. They also partied at clubs in Manhattan together, which was more fun than a college party anyway.

The Bottom line was that Andrea thought Nathan was up to no good at his school, solely because he never brought her there, so in return, she forbade him to visit her when she went off to college. Andrea did the entire freshman orientation that summer at Putnam College and afterwards, she traveled with her mom to visit family in North Carolina, where they stayed until late August.

This meant that because of a misplaced vindictive streak, Nathan and Andrea saw each other perhaps two or three times for the entire summer, though they spoke on the phone nearly every other day. The phone calls were often quarrelsome and would lead to one or the other hanging up in anger. Nathan was outraged that he could not visit her and she was adamant about keeping it that way.

Halfway through the first semester the tables turned and suddenly, Andrea wanted Nathan to come and see her at Putnam; but because of his pride, he refused. He refused on grounds that Andrea was being a bitch and that he wasn't her pawn to move around at her whim, though he eventually gave in but played it as if he was going begrudgingly.

Fake feelings aside, he was actually ecstatic. He really missed her and hadn't had sex in months so he was horny as a sailor on leave. It was quite a change from the frequent sex routine he was accustomed to during their first two years together. He wondered if she felt any different.

He boarded an Atlantic City bus, squeezed into the window seat next to an elderly lady and got comfortable for the three-hour ride. He tried sleeping but the situation was not conducive to catching some shut-eye unless a person was exhausted and Nathan was actually wired. He had an erection for nearly the whole ride as he anticipated the smell of Andrea's skin, the beauty of her lips and the sway in her walk. His boner was embarrassing to have since he was sitting next to an old lady. He got up to use the bathroom and almost poked her eye out.

Once the bus pulled into Atlantic City, Nathan exchanged his ticket for twenty bucks in quarters and be-lined for a pay phone to call Andrea. Her roommate answered and said that Andrea was in class but that he should catch the bus or a cab to the campus and come straight to their dorm. He wrote down the address and directions, played a few slot machines then hailed a cab for the campus.

It was a ten-minute ride to Andrea's dorm room but it felt longer with a cabbie whose mouth was on overdrive. The dude talked for the entire ten minutes but was generally friendly. The cab pulled up and Nathan fetched his bag from the trunk, paid his fare with a tip and knocked on Andrea's dorm door. A perky brunette with juicy tits swung the door open sporting a great smile and a pair of short-shorts. Her name was Hannah and she welcomed Nathan, took his bag and told him Andrea should be back shortly.

She motioned for Nathan to sit on the couch and passed him the remote control for the TV. Nathan, Hannah and the third roommate named Sherry had some small talk about school and the recent snowstorm while waiting for Andrea to return. After fifteen minutes of chitchat they showed Nathan to Andrea's room and he put his bag down by her desk, laid on her bed and before long he was sleeping. He woke up with Andrea standing over him with her ripe breast brushing his face. He instinctively put her nipple into his mouth, which set off a wild session of hot and steamy sex.

Suddenly, it was if nothing had changed. The pre-coital banter was laced with good-natured ribbing and affectionate touching; yet, it was different. It dawned on Nathan how much he'd been missing those moments. He revisited in his mind the bizarre manner in which Andrea suddenly flipped the script and practically begged him to visit her at school, when previously he was persona non-grata. He stifled the urge to bring it up as he basked in a treasured moment.

While Nathan was down at Andrea's school for the weekend, she showed him off like a new Gucci bag. They went to the student center and played pool and video games, after which she snuck him into the cafeteria for dinner. They hung out in her apartment and played drinking games as Andrea introduced Nathan to her friends. They were her new friends and were cool but something felt different.

Perhaps it was the recent time and distance between them but Nathan felt as if he was meeting Andrea again, for the very first time. She felt a bit older, more grown. He still remembers her as a high school girl and though she had only been in college for a few months, it felt like she'd been there forever. Her new friends felt like her old friends and he felt like her new friend.

It was quite the weekend for them both and the recent rupture in their relationship was starting to feel like the distant past. They had incredible "put a sock in your mouth" sex and it was just as good, if not better, than he remembered. The status of their union was broached a few times but not in any detail as the moment was winning out and a discussion of such would only ruin it. Since he was in no mood to wreck it, on they pretended, acting as if nothing was amiss. It was the one thing that had to be talked about, the giant, neon-green elephant in the room that wasn't being acknowledged.

Nathan waited until the day he was leaving to express his feelings about their relationship. He told Andrea how he felt scorned when she banned him from seeing her during the summer and the beginning of the semester. She tried to make it out to be retribution for Nathan's actions during his freshman year in college but Nathan pointed out that it was totally different.

He couldn't see how Andrea was trying to draw a correlation between the two. It was like she was making an excuse for something. It was the only answer to why she was acting so illogical. The conversation began as they lay in bed in the twilight before he was to leave and lasted into the morning. His bus was departing in the afternoon so he saw her off to class as the sun was high in the sky. He said goodbye as he would be gone when she returned.

Never a packer, Nathan rushed to find his belongings, which were strewn around Andrea's bedroom. His sneakers were out in the living room, a few books were under her bed and his soiled underwear was in her closet. He dug through the pile of garments on the bottom of her armoire and found everything besides his prized NY Knicks T-Shirt so he dug deeper and ultimately, stumbled upon an object that ultimately broke the relationship in half.

It was the truth. It was the answers that she was harboring, yet was he really ready for the truth? Sometimes ignorance IS bliss, and it definitely allowed for more weekends like the one he just spent with Andrea. Bliss was the easy route to take when the truth was blunt and painful, as it often is. Nathan wasn't sure he was strong enough. The truth was often too much to digest and if that was the case, Nathan had to decide what he truly sought.

If it was the satisfaction of having his suspicions validated, then perhaps he shouldn't do it; violate the bond of trust and principal of privacy? But hell, it was right there! He knew it was her diary because the book was labeled "Diary" on the front in calligraphy. It was a basic, black, lined composition book clasped with a skinny blue rubber band.

The need to find some answers to why Andrea was acting so bizarre for many months trumped the other thoughts in Nathan's mind, though it didn't win without the arrival of butterflies in his stomach. He knew that looking through the pages would start him down a slippery slope to which, perhaps, he could never return.

Nathan's heart raced. He made a decision to read the diary and would have to live with the consequences of its contents. He stood up from the closet floor, put the diary on the bed, then closed and locked the bedroom door since he didn't want her roommates to catch him invading the essence of Andrea's privacy. Nathan took his sneakers off, climbed up on the bed and opened up the book.

The first few pages of the diary were the usual babble about girlfriends, schoolmates and Andrea's mom and were interesting only because he knew the characters on the pages. Based on her diary, it seemed that her high school was rather cliquish and that Andrea tried to navigate her social life without aligning with any particular group. The diary mentioned many things about the summer program and spoke of the fun that she enjoyed while there.

About twenty pages or so into the diary, Andrea started to show strong animosity towards Nathan. He recognized the feelings that she expressed in the book as the feelings she expressed to him during his ban from her campus and it was as crazy written on pages as it was during her verbal rages.

According to her written words, Nathan was tried and convicted of actions, deeds, and thoughts not of his nature. He was colored a republican in a Dem state but it was untrue! Andrea's perverted view of his character and intentions were like a little kid at adult swim, totally out of place and unwanted. The words rampaged and tore through his emotions on many levels.

The place that she was writing about, which was her life with Nathan, was like an alter universe where Nathan didn't do what he did, what he said he didn't say and what he thought was not truly of his thinking; though proof of it was not available. It read like a bad soap opera, a novella on Spanish television where the cliffhanger was preposterous and the plot made no sense. It would have been entertaining in a goofy way if it wasn't talking about his life. It was the world of a woman, or more like a girl, gone mad. It was clearly leading up to something bad, something that was obviously going to disrupt his life.

Ten minutes into the diary and after a few seconds of panic when he thought her roommates would discover him, Nathan's heart dropped into his boots, his pulse raced and a bit of bile rose to his mouth. Around page thirty, Andrea revealed to her diary that she had an affair. OK, maybe it wasn't an affair, which sounds so "One Life To Live". It wasn't that adult in nature; she simply cheated on him and it confirmed his fears and suspicions. It was with that dorky kid Ed but it didn't happen in the summer, when they were away for the summer together, instead it happened during the school year.

It would have hurt less if it happened during the summer, but instead it happened in her bed; the bed where he lost his virginity. In her diary, Andrea wrote about how Nathan never took her anywhere and never came to see her or pick her up from school. Nathan was angry as he thought to himself that he didn't have a magic carpet or Lear jet to fly to Andrea's school after his classes.

She wrote that Ed picked her up from school a few times and walked her home. Nathan thought that Ed probably took the same route, which was walk down Lincoln Boulevard and turn down Pour Avenue, all the time catching a boner when the wind blew up Andrea's little Catholic school skirt. Nathan was sure that Ed fucked her all day and was then rushed out the apartment right before Andrea's mother came home from work.

Andrea went on to write that she and Ed had sex several times and that she was even thinking about taking Ed to her senior prom. Nathan felt totally outraged about what was taking place in Andrea's diary. It made him angry that she would invite Ed to her graduation party knowing that he was coming. Nathan saw then that Andrea was really stringing him along. He suspected something was going on between Andrea and Ed, but he had no proof.

Nathan also felt embarrassed in retrospect. He had a conversation with Ed after Andrea told him to stop having a bad attitude at her graduation party. Ed probably laughed at him with his friends when they left, Nathan thought. The next year, Nathan found out that he and Ed had common friends and they even smoked pot together on one occasion. Ed probably told those dudes that he banged Nathan's girl and they probably clowned him behind his back, Nathan thought. Nathan thought that they were probably still clowning him, which really made his blood boil.

Nathan was having hot flashes. He was having visions of the consequences of Andrea's actions. Thoughts about how she desecrated the bed where he lost his virginity and how he was played for a fool were running through his head. She did all of this, supposedly, because she thought that Nathan was cheating on her. She wrote in the diary that she was sure Nathan was up at school cheating with girls and it was the reason why he never brought her around. She wrote that he probably had another girlfriend, though there were never any solid grounds for such accusations. Maybe she did feel neglected but she wasn't, she was just left alone more than she was used to.

Nathan wasn't having sex with Andrea as much during his freshman year in college but she had become a beast and obviously would not be denied. It was like Sara all over again. Just because he played the "Sara" hand correctly by breaking up with her before the summer began, didn't mean he had all the answers in every situation. He knew that Sara was a freak and that she wouldn't be faithful to him while he was gone for the summer, but he played it wrong with Andrea. He loved that girl and love made him a fool...........and this was before the second shoe dropped!

Just as he was trying to deal with his feelings about her hooking-up with Ed, Andrea started to write about this other dude in her diary. This didn't start off as sex, it started out on some ole' romantic shit; candle-lit dinners and walks on the beach that past summer. It was a short time removed from the moment that he was reading the actual words. The high school thing was bitter and crushing but the college cheating was recent. It could still be happening Nathan thought. Perhaps it was happening with someone that he might have met down at her college as she was showing him off, Nathan thought

A few pages later, it started to get heavy with the guy. His name was Wally. Nathan's first thought was how dorky the dude Wally sounded. Andrea sure had a knack for picking the craziest dudes with dorky names to sneak around with. Well, she actually didn't sneak around with Wally because they were openly having a relationship. She still mentioned Nathan in the diary but his name became infrequent and weak. She was no longer justifying her actions by Nathan's "cheating", she was just doing. Doing what she wanted to do, when and how she wanted to do it.

Apparently, Wally had a really sick apartment with a balcony that looked out to the beach and a Jacuzzi tub in his bathroom. This guy seemed like a prick. Nathan didn't know him but he could tell that he was a prick. He was a senior in college and using all his knowledge and belongings to his advantage. Not that it's anything wrong with using what you have to get what you want but Nathan could tell it was done in a very prick-like manner. A few pages later, it finally happened! Andrea and Wally had sex on the beach (which was why Nathan never ordered that drink) and it was fireworks and love according to Andrea.

Nathan really wanted to put the book down. Andrea and "Wally" did it a few more times in the subsequent pages, after the initial encounter on the beach, but her entries were coming to an end. The last few pages he read were the words of a confused girl. She didn't know what she was doing. It apparently wasn't working out with that fucking prick Wally, whom Nathan knew would only be in it for the ass.

She suddenly started mentioning Nathan again. In the diary, she started reminiscing about the good times she and Nathan had and started speaking positively about their relationship. Nathan figured it to be around the time that Andrea decided to call him, started to invite him down to see her at college. He was a fool to have ever come. He was a fool to have ever loved her. He was a fool to all of Andrea's friends at school that knew about her and Wally.

Nathan sat there dazed; too hurt to cry and too weak to move, when suddenly everything started going in slow motion. The next moment, perhaps it was a minute or an hour after reading the book; Andrea returned and discovered Nathan with the diary. Her face raced through a range of emotions from stunned to angry to hurt while her eyes welled up like a levee about to breach. Andrea fell to her knees and started crying, first as a whimper, which then grew to uncontrollable wailing and sobbing.

Nathan hopped up and off of the bed, dropped the book at Andrea's feet, and then walked past her and out the door. She ran after Nathan and tried to pull him back into the apartment but Nathan was angry and pushed her down in the snow, where Andrea lay, crying hysterically. He stormed off to the student center, checked the schedule for the next bus to Atlantic City, and played some video games to kill time.

Fifteen minutes later, Andrea's roommates turned up at the student center looking for Nathan. He knew this because they came in the door a bit frantic, looking back and forth through the people that were hanging out downstairs. Luckily, the game room offered a bird's eye view to the front half of the first floor in the student center and being that he really didn't want to deal with any histrionics, Nathan decided to avoid the roommates by taking the back staircase. He came out and ducked down a flight, then ducked into the bookstore. He was in the bookstore entrance when he heard his name called out.

The roommates ran over to him, pantomimed loss of breath and said Andrea had a knife and was threatening to kill herself. They both begged Nathan to come back to the apartment. He looked one girl straight in the eye and said he could care less about Andrea's suicidal tendencies. Only when the roommate reminded Nathan that he left his bag back at the apartment did Nathan agree to return.

On the walk back, Andrea's roommates explained how sorry Andrea felt, but it wasn't the right place for sorry. No matter what was said, all Nathan heard was Andrea moaning in ecstasy as she lay on the beach with Wally. Nathan wondered if Wally had seen him and Andrea gallivanting around campus and if he was snickering about how she was playing him for a fool. Nathan looked at the roommates and felt ashamed because they were in on the whole thing as well. Those girls knew that Andrea had a torrid affair and he felt like a fool in their presence.

It was a remake of that Jim Carrey movie "The Truman Show" and he was the one being suckered like some tool. It stunk being a tool Nathan thought to himself. It's not how he envisioned himself. It made him question how others saw him. Did he look like a tool to the whole world? He was equally mad as embarrassed and didn't want to see her again. He was afraid of how he would manifest all of his roiling emotions.

Nathan wasn't a women beater. Nathan didn't hit kids either, but he felt that it could get crazy in her apartment and he could lose control. Nathan didn't need any craziness in his life, but he felt like he could go a bit Postal. The two roommates entered the apartment with Nathan and found Andrea leaning against the wall with a large chopping knife in her hand.

She was crying uncontrollably and screaming how sorry she was and that she really loved him. Nathan was enraged but restrained from striking Andrea. He surely thought about it though, as he cursed her with extreme venom, calling her every foul name he could think of. When he walked past her to get his bag from the bedroom, Andrea Grabbed Nathan's coat and begged him not to leave her.

Nathan pushed Andrea's back against the wall by her shoulders, placed his mouth really close to her face and announced that it was over. He said he wouldn't piss on her if she was on fire and hoped her never saw her again. Nathan grabbed his bag from Andrea's bedroom and slammed the door behind him when he left the apartment, positive that he would never see her again.

Just as nature takes its course, as do the sand in an hourglass and those were the days of Nathan's life. Nathan eventually took Andrea back after nearly six months of Andrea begging and pleading but the deed was done. He now had a hardened heart and sadly, Nathan never loved the same way again. He never completely gave himself to another woman and it was all the result of his initial experience with love.

Nathan eventually dumped Andrea out of the blue on Valentine's Day after she planned a lovely day. She purchased tickets to a concert and was supposed to spend the weekend with him at his school. At that point, Nathan had transferred to Princeton, was living on campus and really wanted to live the college life. He stayed true to his word and never cheated on Andrea before he dumped her, though he has been faithfully unfaithful to each and every woman since.

CHAPTER 5

On the elevator ride down from his office, Nathan didn't feel sure of his secretary's ability to handle the job that he just assigned her and hoped that the whole thing didn't blow up in his face. His wife was becoming increasingly suspicious of his actions and was checking up on him more often. He actually wasn't sure if she was on to him. Perhaps the things she was doing were consistent with the things that a wife would normally do. Nathan thought that he was projecting guilt and this guilt could then manifest as paranoia and blow his cool.

It must be a side effect to not caring about people's feelings. It had to be the missing empathy gene that's making a return and ricocheting back towards him as paranoia; though the strength to conquer the fear of being discovered stems from the perception of what he could have with Missy.

His digestion of the adulterous situation bore fruit imbued with desire. It was the desire of what he really wanted that drove his actions beyond what he sensed to be the bridge. He was riding beyond the point of what was sensible, and sensible was based on his experiences born from past, similar indiscretions.

He's started to think that Missy could be his destiny. That she's the girl he should had met when he was seventeen years old. It's like all the previous girls were just warm-ups to the real thing. That it would be stupid to lunch on that potential for joy, that definitive chance at happiness and if anything, Nathan was not beyond the basic desire for happiness.

Since he hadn't been lucky enough to ever find that sort of true happiness previously, he didn't know if it made him thirstier or a doubting Thomas when it came to true love. He was leaning towards the former, as all the years of settling had opened his mind to what Missy could mean. What she could bring to his life.

But then again, he voted for Al Gore and thought that global warming was a rap group from Detroit so he's been wrong on more than one occasion. Perhaps the pressure of city living had successfully warped Nathan's brain or maybe it was the numerous single malt scotches, slammed at The White Horse Tavern when it was way past his bedtime. Nathan's wife was his partner in life; or at least that's what the minister said. They shared a life together, and the thought of severing that bond was scary and uncomfortable. It's not like she was doing anything to warrant being shat on, though deception of that order rarely has real justification.

The elevator door opened to a lobby brimming with busy people. It was that type of energy from the lobby that kept Nathan's heart pounding and in turn kept him alive. It drove him to reach for the brass ring, strive when he was devoid of drive. It's like a hundred Red Bulls in a shot glass each morning. It spurred Nathan on, sprung to life in his body like a fully charged lithium battery.

Seconds after Nathan stepped off the elevator someone called out his name from across the busy lobby. He turned his head and saw that it was Clarence, front desk security. He was holding up a package and motioning for Nathan to come to the front desk. Nathan yelled across the lobby that packages should be given to the building services department and in turn, was told by Clarence that it was a personal letter someone dropped at the concierge.

Clarence held up the package to show that it didn't have a floor or company name on the envelope, just Nathan's first and last name in the top right corner. Nathan reiterated that it should be given to building services and if they wouldn't deliver it, he would pick it up when he returned. Nathan walked away before Clarence could respond.

He stopped at the Newspaper Kiosk next to the shoeshine stand, picked up a NY Times and a NY post and headed out the door. The bustle on the street was severe, as a mix of office workers, messengers, tourists and street hustlers shared the same cramped space. He headed up Broadway and popped into a Victoria's Secret emporium just as they were opening the shop.

It was barely anyone inside the store besides the workers and he was greeted by a few, first-shift retail smiles from salesgirls that would have loved to be home in their beds. He offered pleasantries and meandered towards the back, fingering a few frilly garments along the way.

The store brought back memories of Sara; though he never had sex with her during their high school relationship, he did hook up with her on the humble when he was in college. It was the last day of school before winter break and Nathan was waiting for his brother to pick him up. Nathan joked around with a few friends lucky enough to be heading down to Florida for the break and wished he were heading for fun in the sun himself. Nathan's brother pulled up in his car and after getting a few promises of pictures from the beach when the semester resumed, Nathan hopped in the back seat of Justin's Maxima and was passed a smoldering joint before he could get his seat belt on.

When Nathan reminded Justin that he didn't smoke, Justin looked at him like he was an alien and thought for sure Nathan was joking. College had brought about a few changes for Nathan and one of them was giving up weed. He smoked so much of it in high school that the thrill of it had passed. That and the paranoia, which accompanied the high, was enough to make him call it quits with the chronic, though it wasn't until he transferred to Princeton that he totally stopped.

Justin passed it to his friend Mark in the front seat but told him to lower it as they passed campus security. Though they were usually a joke, the campus cops at Nathan's college could be assholes sometimes so it was always best to take precaution in their presence.

Ten minutes into the ride home, Justin told Nathan how he ran into Sara at the Newport Centre Mall in Jersey City and how hot she looked. He said that she was working in Victoria's Secret and that she asked about him incessantly, even though Justin was trying to hook himself up. It didn't bother Nathan that his brother admitted to making a move on his ex-girlfriend, probably because they had never consummated their girlfriend/boyfriend union with sex and therefore it lacked any sort of long-term territorial-ism.

Justin asked, after the fact, if Nathan would have been sore had he hooked up with Sara, which was a question that didn't have an easy answer. Not that it mattered because in reality, Nathan really didn't give a shit. He hadn't thought about Sara in quite a while but after Justin brought it up, Austin thought about her several times while he was home. He was off from school for a month and started to get jelly of the other kids that were down in Florida, frolicking on the beach. He visited some friends, played basketball and went to a few parties but he mostly lounged around and did nothing.

The third Saturday of the break, Justin called Nathan and asked if he wanted to ride to the Newport Centre Mall and check out Sara. Nathan responded with an affirmative yes and showered quickly, hoping to get out of the house before his mother returned from the supermarket and burdened him with Saturday errands and chores.

He heard Justin's horn and ran out the house just as his mom pulled up. Nathan assured her that he would do anything she wanted him to do when he returned and then hopped in the back seat of Justin's car. Mark was in his usual shotgun position in the front, working the radio and talking endless shit about people that Nathan didn't know.

Once at the mall, they mapped a plan of action to accomplish the tasks at hand. Mark wanted to peep the new Jordan's at Footlocker and Athletes Foot, which where both on the second floor. Justin was bound for the food court to satisfy his munchies and Nathan was headed for Victoria's Secret. They all split up on separate missions but the plan was to meet at Ms. Fields Cookies in an hour.

Justin was the only one with a cell phone, so if all else failed they could call him from a pay phone. Nathan hoped that being high would not hinder Justin's ability to hear his phone. This was of extreme importance since Justin drove to the mall and he was known to leave people stranded if he got a booty call or anything that had the slightest potential of being one.

On the ride up the escalator, Nathan thought about what he would say to Sara after three years. It wasn't awkward like a twenty-year high school reunion, where everyone's change was dramatic after so much time, but he was a bit jittery since his last memory of her wasn't good. He dumped Sara at the start of the summer after his sophomore year in high school. He was going away to a summer program until mid-August and Sara was the horniest girl he had ever met. Only a fool would attempt to hold down a long distance relationship with her and set himself up to be the sucker of the school come September.

It was just his good fortune to have her sit behind him in Home Room for his junior year in high school. Sara and her cousin Eva, who also shared the same homeroom, tortured Nathan every chance they got. Sara sat in the desk immediately behind Nathan's and kicked his chair every day, called him every name imaginable and threatened him with bodily harm. The debris that was really stuck in Sara's craw was that they never had sex. It was an inverse to the natural scenario of a teenage boy applying pressure to a teenage girl to get naked and get it on and his disappointment if he never got a chance to "hit it".

Sara was the horn dog in the relationship, and though Nathan wanted to sex her, something told him that it wasn't right. Was he too cautious? Perhaps! But it made for surreal moments of Sara begging Nathan to fuck her. Her high-pitched, cartoonish voice would cry like a cat in heat and her beautifully big eyes would tear up whenever Nathan denied her dick. It was almost weird and would almost work but Nathan always stuck to his guns. That relationship made him realize the power that the dick wielded over girls, and later, over women. It was the first time that a girl begged Nathan to fuck her, but it wouldn't be the last.

A stroke of luck removed Nathan from that Homeroom after he was placed in an experimental program for advanced students, so for the last two years of high school, he didn't see much of Sara. When he did see her, he tried to stand still like a Praying Mantis lest she spot him and erupt in teen female rage. Luckily, Nathan got through the rest of his high school years unscathed and never saw Sara again after they graduated.

The second floor of the Mall was very crowded and as he approached Victoria's Secrets, Nathan thought he saw a girl that looked just like Sara in The Limited, a woman's clothing store adjacent to Vickie Secrets. He popped in the store for a bit of faux browsing and after a few minutes he saw the girl again and it was Sara. He walked up from behind and put his hands over her eyes and said, "guess who". She didn't say a word, so he repeated, "guess who", which was met by more silence.

He felt kind of stupid at that point, like she was going to turn around and smack his face or tell security that he had fondled her breast. Nathan removed his hands and stepped back cautiously as Sara turned around to face him. Instead of anger Sara smiled broadly and let out a high-pitched squeal, which startled a few customers. She threw her arms around his neck and levitated herself off of the floor, which waylaid his fears.

Sara was wearing just what he last remembered her in and hadn't changed much. It occurred to him now, after a few years removed from high school that she looked kind of tart-ish, like she was dressed for a music video every day. She was still fond of miniskirts and little tube tops and even though it was the dead of winter outside, she was dressed like it was early July. She motioned for Nathan to follow her through a passageway that led to Victoria's Secret.

She headed to the back of the store, grabbed a little teddy off the rack held it to her body and asked Nathan how she would look in it. Before he could answer, she grabbed another item, this one a little French maid number and did the same thing. Nathan smiled and said that both looked great, then turned around and grabbed one himself, held it up to his body and asked the same question.

She squealed again, grabbed him and gave him a deep, wet kiss that was totally inappropriate for the work place. Nathan felt a bit embarrassed and looked around a bit sheepishly. He followed her around the store as she folded and re-hung itsy bitsy garments while they engaged in catch-up chitchat.

Sara told Nathan that she was seeing some dude in the Navy who was stationed nearby at the naval base in Staten Island and that they recently shacked up together. Nathan felt a bit sad for the Navy dude because he knew that Sara was likely cheating on him and wondered if he was knowingly cuckold or even if you could be cuckold without knowing it. She also mentioned her diabolical cousin Eva and that she was married with a baby and had moved down to Virginia.

Conversation, squeals and neglected customers eventually materialized the store manager, who told Sara to get back to work. After the third time that the manager found them talking and Sara not working, Nathan suggested that he and Sara exchange phone numbers so she could take care of the customers. They made plans to go out while he was home for the winter break, shared another wet and sloppy sex kiss and then Nathan headed for the door. Sara's manager caught up with him at the doorway and pulled him aside.

Nathan had no idea what she was going to say but it surely involved Sara. She took umbrage with Sara not heeding her words about slacking off and felt like she let her slide way too much. Nathan thought that she was self-conscious about looking like a pushover. The manager said that she was a bit easy on her because Sara was one of the top selling sales girls in the limited brand stores for the NYC metro area. She said that Sara had a way of making guys leave the store with so many items that it was like hoodoo! It's something she's saying, either verbally or with her body language, which makes men want to buy things for their girlfriends, the manager said.

Some of the guys would even buy Sara stuff, the manager said. They would have it gift wrapped and left at the counter for Sara to pick up. Nathan saw that the manager was exploiting Sara's sexuality to sell more clothes, which was normal. Everybody gets exploited for his or her value in America Nathan thought. It's the American way! In another place and time, a girl like Sara could be a call girl or prostitute or maybe used as bait by grifters. Perhaps she was lucky that her exploitation was by the Limited Brand and not Guido the Killer Pimp, Nathan thought to himself!

Because of lousy timing, Nathan and Sara never hooked up while he was home on break, so instead it was planned for Sara to come visit Nathan when he went back to school. A few weeks after the second semester had begun, Nathan got a call from Sara on a Wednesday afternoon while he was still lying in bed. She sounded real excited and wanted to come see him that weekend, and although he had lots of studying to do, he said yes anyway.

The Friday that Sara was going to visit Nathan, he went to a party on campus that was close to the train depot. He was dancing and drinking some beers that he and his friends snuck into the party. Nathan realized the time and had his friend Tim drive him to the station to scoop Sara but she was not at the station when the train arrived. He waited for the next train and when she wasn't on that one either, he and Tim went back to the party to pick up where they left off. He figured that she had to cancel for some reason and felt that he gave it the ole "college try" by waiting for a half-hour at the station.

After the party, Nathan was dropped off at his dormitory with a bag full of White Castle Fish Sandwiches, fries, a chocolate shake and visions of sleep in his head. He had a great time at the party; met a few girls, got some phone numbers and chugged a few beers. It was a perfect night if he had to say so. We'll, not so perfect because he went home alone, but still, relatively speaking, not so bad. He opened the door to his dorm room and could see the light of his answering machine flickering in the dark and that quite a few messages had been left.

He pressed play and heard Sara's high pitched voice curling out of the machine and knew that the other messages was surely from her as well. Before he could get through the entire message, his phone rang and it was Sara on the line. Apparently, Sara did come but was an hour late to meet him. She was still at the train station and was pissed off that she had to wait in the cold.

He was sure that she was dressed inappropriately for the weather, because she was always dressed inappropriately for the weather, so instead of finding someone to go and pick her up, he told her to get a cab and that he would pay for it. After Nathan gave Sara his address, she hung up the phone without saying goodbye and twenty minutes later she was at his door.

She came into Nathan's room with a scowl on her face that was quite scary. She plopped her overnight bag down on

Nathan's bed, pulled out the chair from his desk, sat down, crossed her legs and declared that she was pissed off. Nathan explained that he went to the train station, didn't see her, waited for the next train and when he still didn't see her, he figured that she couldn't make it.

Yes it was true that he could have went back to his room to see if she called or at least checked his voicemail from the party to see if she left a message, so he apologized. Nathan said that he was sorry and that he accepted full responsibility for the whole thing. She pouted for five more minutes and then suddenly she stopped.

She took her coat off, and just as Nathan figured, she was dressed like she was on Venice Beach. She was wearing a red frilly miniskirt with fishnet stockings, powder blue pump heels and a sheer button down blouse that was tied around her waist at the bottom. He could easily see that she didn't have on a bra, as her areola and nipples were still perked up from the frigid weather.

Long story short was that Sara proceeded to give Nathan a firsthand glimpse into the operations of a Nymphomaniac. The first thing she did was un-zip his pants and gave him the type of blow job that a man typically had to pay for. It ended with a scream, in a pitch, which Nathan had never reached. He trembled even though he tried not to and when he looked down, Sara was licking her lips while looking into his eyes. There was not a trace of his load to be found because Sara had slurped it down like a mango slushy. It was Nathan's first experience with a woman "swallowing"; and he liked it!

She then got up off her knees, walked over to Nathan's bed and grabbed her bag. She excused herself to go to the bathroom and when she closed the door behind her, Nathan collapsed on the bed in post-nut bliss! He lay there with a silly smile plastered across his face for an indeterminate amount of time until he was jolted back into the moment by the closing of his room door. He sat up to see Sara standing there in a crazy French Maid teddy; the same one from Victoria's secrets that he liked. From that point on the story became quite redundant, as it was all bang, bang, bang and skeet, skeet, skeet.

Each time that they finished, Sara was back fondling him minutes later, cajoling his cock to raise up for yet another round. By the eighth time, Nathan was shooting puppy water and his dick was suffering from friction burn. Sara was completely insatiable and it crossed his mind that, perhaps he should set her out for a few friends to enjoy. It seemed that she could take on a whole football team and come out the victor.

She would squeal in such delight and concentrated sexual enjoyment that it started to feel a bit tawdry. He was but a tool for her enjoyment, and he was no one's tool! He started to feel used, and after three packs of condoms, several hours of animal loving and a tenth ejaculation that yielded nothing more than cloudy soymilk, Nathan called it quits. He actually did it for his sanity and well being.

Friday night had turned into Saturday evening and he was completely drained. She sucked and fucked every drop of life from Nathan's body and it was nothing left for him to do but to send her home. There's nothing really to be said to a girl like Sara after a night like that. He told her that he had school obligations and really needed to study for a few upcoming exams and that she would have to leave.

Sara started crying, hid under the covers and refused to budge and it took Nathan more than an hour to convince her he wasn't just getting rid of her. He showed Sara his syllabi, assignment sheets and how much reading he had to finish before the exams and she finally relented, but not before he gave her a tour of the campus.

As they walked and talked it became crystalline that they had nothing in common and how different their lives were going a mere three years out of high school. He kissed her as she boarded the campus bus and that was the last that he ever saw of Sara, but her memory always permeated his thoughts whenever he walked into a Vicky Secrets. Sara had actually burned an indelible impression in his brain because whenever he wants to bring about a freaky, kinky sexual romp, he always buys a girl that very same French Maid teddy. Which was why he was in the store that day; he wanted to take the relationship with Missy to another level.

CHAPTER 6

In Nathan's mind, he was at a point with Missy where it was either going to wreck his marriage or it would get reduced to yet another mindless fling. The mindless fling made more sense since the mindless fling was Nathan's forte. He was quite adept at keeping those little flings a secret. The real problem was the fling that turns into something more, that morphs into something that was harder to deal with. Nathan thought that the thing with Missy could easily turn into a difficult situation and he didn't need a difficult situation. If he could slut this girl up, start treating her like a cheap hooker, then maybe the relationship would become nothing more than hot sex on a platter.

Nathan looked through a few racks of clothes and then asked the doe-eyed sales clerk if she could find him the French Maid teddy. She told him that, unfortunately, Victoria's Secret had decided to stop selling that particular item because it didn't fit in with the brand concept. Upon asking why, she told him, quite frankly, that it was a bit tacky for Victoria's Secret and was more for a store like Fredrick's Of Hollywood or Agent Provocateur. Nathan asked for the directions to either one of those places, in which case the previously super informed sales girl suddenly started drawing blanks. He thanked her and walked out of the store.

The options with Missy, if things kept going in the same direction, left a bad taste in Nathan's mouth. Then again, the bad taste in his mouth could have come from the foul aroma of bacon that enveloped the corner deli that he was stepping into. He paused and debated at the door of the store whether to enter. He could easily get what he wanted in another deli that didn't reek of bacon and butter.

Since cigarettes are sold in nearly every store on Broadway, he pivoted around to exit the stench and suddenly had hot liquid on his chest. He recoiled with a mild yelp and looked down to see an old lady with bright red lipstick holding a large cup of Starbucks coffee in a trembling, liver spotted hand. He walked over to the counter and was followed by the apologetic old lady. He grabbed a handful of napkins and vainly dabbed at his shirt, which was ruined for the day.

After an uncomfortable moment with the old lady rubbing his chest with a saliva-soaked napkin and apologizing in Yiddish, Nathan bought a pack of smokes, removed his shirt and headed out the door towards the French Cleaners. He was a little pissed off but nothing major. His frequent lunchtime dalliances had led to soiled garments that needed immediate dry cleaning and Ito at the French Cleaners had helped him out of many tight spots and always came through with flying colors.

Ito took the soiled garment and filled out the dry cleaning slip without Nathan having to utter a word and told him that his shirt would be ready at 5pm. When Ito handed the slip to Nathan, he gave him a smile that confused Nathan. It was kind of eerie, like the look in a horror movie before something happens. Nathan couldn't recall that look from Ito before. Ito never passed judgment on the condoms he found in Nathan's coat pockets or the lipstick marks on his shirts so Nathan didn't quite know how to take it. He put the ticket in his pants pocket, smiled and pushed the door marked "exit".

Now shirtless before his day had even begun, another "to do" had been added to his list and shot straight to the top; since prancing around all day without a shirt was not an option. Nathan wished that he hadn't wore his AC/DC Tee underneath his button down and tie but he knew that Missy was bonkers for the band and whatever got her worked up was worth the trouble. He received a few randomly puzzled looks from people, mostly acquaintances actually. The looks came from people that he didn't really know but often nodded his head at on the train or in the elevator.

After several closed stores, Nathan realized that it was too early for the men's clothing stores and boutiques to be open. He'd had to wait another ninety minutes before he could buy a shirt, at least according to the hours posted on most of the boutique doors. Nathan window shopped for a few minutes but in reality, all he needed was a simple button down shirt to which any of the stores on Broadway could provide.

Faced with a bit of downtime, Nathan remembered that he really needed a wireless headset to wear while driving. He usually eschews the clumsiness of an ear piece but he had recently received two traffic tickets for talking on his cell phone while driving and both Missy and his wife complained incessantly when they were in the passenger seat. He peeped into the window of the Cingular store and noticed a handful of new phones on display. Most were of the same sort, either super sleek and slim or small but wider and full of features. Though a few of the phones were James Bonds sexy, Nathan was still stuck on his blackberry. He couldn't live without it actually, in a crackberry sort of way!

He entered the Cingular store and was directed to sign in by a ragged security guy. Nathan was a bit irked because he didn't feel like signing in and though he tried not to reveal that he had an attitude, it shone through nonetheless. Nathan said that he was simply looking for a wireless headset and didn't need any special attention, as he looked around the store. He was directed to a spry and perky sales rep who said, right away, that she would be "happy to help him" while smiling like she recently won the "power-ball" lottery and hadn't told a soul. After asking about the type of ear piece that he was looking for and what environment he would be using it in, she decided that one of the bulkier pieces would best suit his needs.

The sales rep was adamant that the most expensive Motorola headpiece would serve Nathan best, based on his driving style, which was often top down and heavy on the pedal. The Motorola model had the best feature to guard against the wind, the sales rep stated, though Nathan figured that the best feature, in the eyes of the sales rep, was that it was the most expensive model in the store.

Truth be told, he did have problems with other headsets while driving down the highway with the wind flapping his tie and hair. Though it's probably his best choice, he still inquired about a rebate or a preferred customer discount before plunking down his card, as he hated to feel like he was "sold" something.

While ringing up the sale, the cashier mentioned that she really liked his purchase with a shy smile. Nathan seized the moment as a chance for some self-amusement, so he chatted the girl up about his backstage "partying" with ACDC after a crazy performance in Mexico. Turned out that the cashier was Mexican and proceeded to grill Nathan on a litany of details, which triggered his Jedi answer tactics.

Those Jedi answer tactics were a by-product of his corporate Machiavellianism, and were subconsciously unleashed in those situations. Every question was met with a question, with a few generic details, which begot an answer from the person asking the question.

Example:

Cashier

"Oh my god, where did you see them perform?"

Nathan

"At that huuuge stadium down there, the really nice one"

Cashier

"Estadio Azteca?"

Nathan

"Yeah, I think that was the one, it was huge"

Cashier

"The one that's built over the old volcano?"

Nathan

"Yeah, that one…it was great!"

Cashier

"I'm so jealous, was it crazy backstage?"

Nathan

"I couldn't begin to tell you, it's too early in the day"

Cashier

"You're so lucky"

Nathan smiled and thanked the girl for the headset and stuffed the receipt in his front right pocket, which felt bulky and uncomfortable. Nathan put the bag on the counter, removed his car keys from his front left pocket, and placed it next to his bag. As the Porsche key grabbed her attention, Nathan flashed his Gucci emblazoned money clip and switched that to his left front pocket. He then returned the Porsche key to the pocket it was removed from; the front left pocket.

Now he had his money clip and his car key in his front left pocket and his receipt in his front right pocket and it didn't mean anything at all. It was a bunch of nothing, though actually it was good for something, as it successfully put *her* in his pocket.

After the sleight of hand and hi-wire slick-talk was skillfully performed, without a net, Nathan grabbed the bag, gave the cashiers manicured fingers a slight squeeze and wished her a lovely day. He turned and headed for the door and could see the reflection of the girl digesting the moment as she filled her eyes with his departing image. He made a mental note to return the headset to the store within a week, along with a dinner invitation for the sales girl.

It was similar, in essence, to the way that he reeled in Missy, but it was almost the total opposite. He spun a very similar web of measured actions and clever verbosity that Missy ducked like a Mike Tyson punch. She cut through the crap and called out his game in a quick instance, which Nathan found incredibly sexy.

Like a stern schoolteacher that looked hot in a short skirt, Missy pulled his card and poked through his entanglement. Luckily, most women weren't like Missy and more like the cashier. Though it was sexy how Missy shot Nathan's game down, he definitely liked when his game ran unabated, especially since most girls weren't 't as hot as Missy and wouldn't be so sexy shooting him down.

One of the things that Nathan liked about Missy was that she wasn't his wife. Though one woman could and should be a wife, mother, partner and vixen, Missy could be his professional lover. She need not apply for any other position. Certainly not mother, since he had a kid and didn't desire another and he thought that being a partner was way overrated unless you were a cop or on Dancing With The Stars. He could keep the relationship with Missy fresh and exciting without any drawbacks.

Though he was drifting on the dream and that thought, he was still indifferent to the question of why. Why did he feel the need to act on urges that many people suppress? He was raised in a splintered family so he knew the negative effect that such a situation could have on a child. He knew that it would be unfair to put his kid through something that he had first hand, negative experience with, but still; there was something about Missy. He knew that he was getting ahead of himself a bit because it was totally premature to throw over Jacqueline with such haste. He refocused on the goal of the day, which was to gauge where his relationship with Missy was going.

It was still an hour before the boutiques would open for him to buy a new shirt, so with time to kill, Nathan decided to head over to the parking garage and pick up his car. He always parked it in the garage and brought it out on the weekends and a few times during the week in the summer. It was fast, sleek, topless and red, but more importantly it was a magnet for women, mostly because it' was fast, sleek, topless and red.

The car comforted him when he drove it and was a badge of his success that validated his worth, though he would only admit such a shallow feeling to himself when drunk and debating whether to pick it up from the garage. Prior to the Porsche, Nathan rode a motorcycle, though Jacqueline nagged him about its danger after Catherine was born. She said that a motorcycle was for single men, not a married man with a newborn baby girl and he knew that Jacqueline was right.

He sold the bike and stepped up to the Porsche 911 Carrera Cabriolet 4S a few months back, though he was only allowed to buy it if he got Jackie something more sensible, which turned out to be a Volvo station wagon. The Volvo station wagon was not only sensible but also the safest car on the road, which appeased the parent in both Jackie and Nathan. So he had to spend an extra Forty Thousand dollars to get his red and topless Porsche but it was worth every buck.

CHAPTER 7

He hailed a cab outside of the Cingular store and as
Nathan hopped in he could see the cashier looking through the

door as he pulled away. Nathan thought that she probably doubted he even had a Porsche since he hopped in a cab, so he made another mental note to drive up to the store and park it right outside when he returned. The cab driver was named Islam. Nathan made a note of the cabby's name each time he took a cab, which was mainly for conversation purposes. He enjoyed the brief taxi banter, even though the topics were mostly the same, i.e. weather, traffic, if business was slow, the Yankees and women.

Women seemed to be the favorite topic of many cabbies, bordering on obsessive in some cases. Perhaps it was the freedom of American women compared to a cabby's home country or his freedom from censure and public decorum in New York City. Once Nathan initiated the conversation, Islam rushed through the weather (good), business (slow) and the Yankee's (love Derek Jeter) and settled on a woman crossing in front of the cab at a red light.

Islam
"I love the women in the high heels"
Nathan
"Oh you like that?"
Islam
"Yes, very much"
Nathan
"Me to my friend, especially when the weather is nice"
Islam
"Yes, yes I like that too"
Nathan
"You like a woman to wear high heels during sex?"
Islam
"Excuse me?"
Nathan
"During sex, it's great when she keeps the pumps on"
Islam
"I've never had that sir, I don't know much about it"
Nathan

"You should try it"
Islam
*"Well my wife won't be comfortable like that and she doesn't own
any high heel shoes"*
Nathan
"Well not with your wife, with some other women"
Islam
"Excuse me sir, but I don't do that"
Nathan
"Oh, I just thought that"
Islam
"I admire sir, it's nothing wrong with admiring is it"
Nathan
"Not at all Islam, I just thought"
Islam
"That I was like you?"
Nathan
"Well, not like me?"
Islam
"But that I have sex with women other than my wife?"
Nathan
"Well you talked like it"
Islam
"I talk because I admire sir"
Nathan
"I see"

With that, Nathan leaned back in his seat and didn't speak
for a few minutes. Islam asked Nathan if he wouldn't mind
walking from the corner because the traffic was tight and it would
allow him to continue uptown. When Islam asked Nathan that
question, he had no idea that he had touched on a hot-button
subject or what it would lead to. It was a personal pet peeve of
Nathan and it set him off on a tangent.

Nathan ranted and raved that the taxi was there for his
convenience and not the other way around. If he wanted to walk

from the corner, Nathan said he would have taken the subway instead and that service to the door of his destination was expected. He told Islam that he would not accept walking from the corner at all and that he was willing to sit in the traffic for extra time if need be.

Nathan's explosive outburst had merit, though its fiery delivery began the classic Cabby-vs-Customer argument that was endemic to New York City. It was the kind of street beef that could lead to fisticuffs and the need for police intervention. Resolution wasn't easy as Nathan threatened not to pay the fare if he was not delivered to his destination, which infuriated Islam. Holding his ground, Islam stated several times that he wasn't Nathan's servant and that the corner should be good enough, considering the traffic.

Once he realized that getting dropped off at his address could actually take forever, Nathan acquiesced, opened the curbside door and hopped out. Winning the argument was not worth the indeterminate, torturous minutes of hell, so he asked for his receipt and stepped out of the cab. He handed the driver the exact amount + a nickel through the front passenger side window and turned to walk away. Two seconds later he felt the Nickel strike him in the back and turned around to see Islam rolling up the passenger side window and locking the doors.

Nathan picked up the nickel and from the wind-up motion of a baseball pitcher, threw it back at the cab with as much velocity as he could muster. It pinged off the window on the front passenger side and left a small divot in the glass. Islam immediately jumped out and walked angrily around the cab towards Nathan who held his ground with his fists tightly balled. In seconds they were in each other's face, doing the street-fight face dance that usually precipitates either the initial blow, a sensible de-escalation of the situation or, as in that moment, the "fuck you" chest push.

After a series of three "fuck you" chest pushes, passersby separated the two before it turned into a full-blown melee and Nathan backed off while loudly cursing Islam about his offensive body odor and stinky cab. Nathan cut through the small throng of people on the corner that had gathered to watch the spectacle he created and headed down the street towards the parking garage to retrieve his car. Several people pointed him out to their friends and made comments and prognostications on who would have been the victor if the fight would have gone down.

Street-Fight watching is a common social occurrence in NYC. It bonds bike messengers, office workers and UPS drivers with ladies of leisure, panhandlers and business leaders. The mere raising of voices could gather a crowd on any given street, whether uptown or downtown, to see if fists would start to fly. Street-fight watching is distantly related to rubber necking on the highway and both are guilty pleasures best enjoyed in passing, without gaining any real attachment to the situation. The downside for Nathan was that his adrenaline had begun to flow and his heart had started to race but he lost the opportunity for a release.

He passed by a large window and looked at himself in the mirror and didn't see a business executive, but instead he saw a rather angry looking dude in a partially stained ACDC T-shirt. He wondered if his appearance had anything to do with the way the cab driver reacted to him. Either way, Nathan had a major chip on his shoulder and he took it with him into the parking garage. On his way in, he could hear voices on the side of the building and also smelled the distinctive aroma of high-grade weed smoke wafting through the air.

When Nathan got to the booth it was bereft of attendants. He looked around for a few seconds and then rang the bell on the inside of the booth, which was rather loud and reverberated through the garage. He gave it another quick ring and then sat down on the bench next to the empty booth. Nearly a full minute went by before someone showed up, and during that time, Nathan had succeeded in working himself up into quite another angry lather. He was silently seething about the lackadaisical service and let it out as soon as the first employee appeared.

The garage worker was wearing black pants and a white shirt with a red vest over it. He looked to be of Indian or Pakistani descent and had a thick, black mustache and a basic, safe haircut. When he closed the door to the booth and turned around, Nathan was standing there, with his face close to the booth cage, asking why it took so long to receive service. The worker, whose name badge said Sam, looked on with slight indifference as Nathan fussed about fast service for people in a rush. In possession of a wonderfully stoic face that was devoid of any expression, Sam heard out the grievance and when Nathan's tirade ended, asked for the name on the parking space.

This further enraged Nathan as Sam refused to get emotional, which deprived Nathan of an outlet for his displaced anger carried over from the taxicab mishap with Islam. Nathan tossed his driver's license onto the counter of the booth, which was intended to spark a reaction from Sam, though Sam still refused to be baited. He turned around and opened a long cabinet, which had a row of pegs holding many sets of keys and asked Nathan what kind of car he drove. Nathan yelled out "Porsche, a red 911 Porsche" to Sam and said it with extreme insolence.

A few moments passed before Sam turned around and announced that he could not find the keys, which nearly brought Nathan's blood to a boil. He referenced Sam's stupidity, the mental capacity of his mother and the general ineptitude of the garage and promised to take his business elsewhere.

After his outburst was met with another deadpan face from Sam, Nathan demanded to speak to Jorge who was the guy he normally dealt with. Jorge was on a break and wouldn't be back for ten more minutes Sam told Nathan, which threw Nathan fully overboard. He put his finger through the caging and rattled the booth, which made Sam take a step back.

Just as Nathan was about to release another string of invectives, he felt a tap on his left shoulder blade. He whisked around with a deranged demeanor, his face contorted with anger, and saw that a small line had formed behind him. The next person in line, who had tapped him on the shoulder, was an old lady.

She told Nathan that he should calm down and stop causing such a commotion. The old lady from the garage reminded Nathan of the old lady from the deli who spilled coffee all over his shirt, which caused more displaced anger to well up in his throat. It was about to exit his throat as bile and four letter words, when Nathan was interrupted by Sam

Sam
"Mr. Collier, could you please take back your driver's license and move aside so other people can get their cars out of the garage"
Nathan
"(sarcastically) you know Sam, I certainly can, I certainly can Sam"
Sam
"Thank you Mr. Collier"
Nathan
"No problem Sam, I'm glad I could be of help to you………I came in to get my car and I have to be of help to you"

Nathan said this while giving the people behind him a look of disbelief, but he received not one iota of sympathy from anyone as most had already labeled him an asshole. He sat down on the bench with a loud sigh and pulled out his Blackberry. Through all of the excitement he didn't feel it vibrate with the five emails messages that were waiting. He opened the first email with trepidation, as it was from his secretary and may have contained unbearable news of some miscue on her part; like relaying the wrong information to Jacqueline regarding his whereabouts.

Just as he thought, it was a miscue from his secretary though it didn't involve his wife. It was something about a manager from one of his accounts and also about a problem with his car insurance. The next few were not urgent and could wait until he was back in the office, though out of sheer habit he started to compose a reply to the next one that he read. Midway through and after fumbling around for the right words, he decided to stick with his instincts and leave replies until later. Just as he was about to open the last email, which was from an unknown address, he heard Sam call out to somebody.

Walking up the ramp, which Nathan thought was totally unsafe, was Jorge and another worker that Nathan didn't recognize. They were having quite the funny conversation Nathan thought as they both laughed continuously while patting each other on the back. Once they arrived at the booth, Sam pulled Jorge to the side and spoke sternly in his ear. Jorge replied with a shrug of his shoulders and walked back into the booth with Sam, who called Nathan over from the bench. When Nathan cut through the customer line he got a few funny looks, no doubt residual feelings from his earlier outburst.

When he got to the front, Sam pointed to Nathan and asked Jorge to find the Porsche car keys. Jorge smiled and said hello, though Nathan wasn't in the mood for small talk. He reached into his pocket, pulled out his driver's license and handed it over the counter to Jorge, whose hands revealed unmistakable marks of drug usage. There were little burn marks on the tips of his fingers, which were tell tale signs of smoking refer and when Nathan looked into Jorge's eyes, they were glassy and dilated.

Whatever calm Nathan achieved while sitting on the bench was quickly replaced by steam coming out of his ears and foam at his mouth once it dawned on him that Jorge and his buddy were the source of the refer smoke that he smelled while on his way into the building. He snapped his blackberry back into its holster and asked for the manager. Jorge pointed to Sam, who fumbled around in the pocket of his vest and pulled out a manager name tag and pinned it on his chest. The situation would have almost been comical if Nathan weren't so angry.

At that moment, Jorge's Chronic smoking companion stepped into the booth to pick up the slack, as there was a significant crowd of people waiting to pick up their vehicles. Nathan motioned for Sam to come to the end of the booth near the bench to continue the conversation and Sam surely thought it was for Nathan to further voice his displeasure. Sam ventured over and before he could get a word out, Nathan began to apologize for his past behavior. "I came in here angry from other things and unleashed it on you and I'm sorry" Nathan said to Sam, who had a look of surprise on his face.

Nathan had quickly surmised that it wasn't wise to develop an antagonistic relationship in that situation; that's unless he planned on changing to another garage, which though he threatened it, he had no plans on doing. Nathan asked, if, from this point on, Sam could take care of his car when it's at the parking garage. He told Sam that normally he's even keeled and not so high-strung and chalked it up to his shitty day. Sam thought about it for a few seconds, agreed to take care of his car and apologized for the unusual delay and sealed the deal by shaking fingers through the gate of the booth.

Sam had been transferred into the garage from Brooklyn and told Nathan that it was his first week and that he was still learning the ropes and the customers. Nathan said that he usually didn't dress so casual for work. He explained to Sam that his calamitous day had left him in a partially stained ACDC T-shirt and that he actually was in a hurry to find a boutique and buy a proper button down. Sam said that he understood but when he turned around to have Jorge locate the keys, it was only Jorge's cannabis companion in the booth and a line of customers waiting for their cars.

Nathan was really big on customer service and keeping the customer happy. It had been a defining tenant in his career and he projected that onto situations whenever he was a customer. It wasn't overly demanding to want access to his car whenever he came to the garage Nathan thought to himself as he felt slight remorse for his earlier actions.

It was expected for each wo
rker to be knowledgeable of all aspects of such a simple operation; the location of his car included, Nathan thought as the sounds of screeching wheels and stop and go erratic driving echoed back and forth in the garage. It's a twenty-four hour facility and if he showed up at 2am, someone should be right there to fetch his ride Nathan thought.

That he wasn't able to get his car right away, especially since he was the only customer in the garage when he first entered, was bad enough for Nathan. The fact that his delay was the product of a "weed break" by garage employees just compounded the issue. It probably wouldn't have been so upsetting if he hadn't just encountered the same type of customer service breakdown with Islam, the irate cabby.
The sounds of bad driving continued and lightened the air as customers joked about it and were thankful that it wasn't their car that was sputtering down the ramp. That brought a smile to Nathan's face as well, which was quickly replaced by the look of horror. Since none of the customers had been waited on and Jorge was the only worker missing, it dawned on him that the car whose gears were being ruined could be his.

Sam and Nathan looked at each other simultaneously with the same thought and then Sam quickly excused himself and started a brisk walk up the ramp towards the sound of the bad driving. Suddenly a jarring crash turned the garage silent and caused Sam to break into a full jog up the hill. Ten seconds or so after Sam disappeared around the bend, the sound of his screaming voice was heard and then the sound of a car door slamming

Nathan broke towards the ramp at full speed, with his heart racing and his mind flashing images of his lovely red Porsche wrecked by Jorge. The five speed manual transmission on his car could be a little difficult to operate at times, especially if you weren't used to it and more so while under the influence of drugs or alcohol. He knew this because whenever he drove while impaired, which happened more than a few times, the difficulty of working the gears increased exponentially by the amount of intoxicants ingested and it looked and smelled like Jorge smoked an entire spliff while on break.

The door opened and closed again and the sound of the car moving down the ramp with normal movements replaced the deafening sound of his engine being shredded. Before Nathan got to the ramp, his car appeared sporting a minor bruise to the left headlight.

It wasn't anything major, but Nathan could see it from thirty feet away and he wasn't happy. His eyes started to see red and not just from looking at the car. When it stopped right in front of Nathan, Sam had the look of a man who wanted to evaporate into thin air. Sam opened the car door and stepped out, yet before he could say a word, Nathan let out a loud, guttural scream and a spewed a slew of four letter words.

He called out Jorge's name and started up the ramp but was intercepted by Sam. That was the moment that could really change Nathan's day as he had every intention to ring Jorge's neck and pound the weed smoke out of his lungs. When Nathan turned the corner he could see Jorge at the top running away and he gave chase. Sam was running right beside him and pleaded for Nathan not to do anything rash. He guaranteed that the garage's insurance would cover the accident and would also give Nathan a few months of free parking, but that accosting Jorge was not the answer

Not for nothing, but Nathan was beyond reasoning; way past it. His fumbling secretary, the clumsy old woman who spilled coffee on his shirt and Islam the taxi driver had joined together in a huge brain boil and Jorge was the lance, which pierced and leaked a toxic puss that contaminated his mind. He ran up the ramp to the top landing and saw Jorge on the far end, trying to hide behind a Cadillac truck. Nathan ran with destruction in his blood and was intercepted by Sam, again, who pleaded with him to calm down.

When Nathan reached the Cadillac, Jorge started apologizing about denting his car and said he didn't want any trouble as he eluded Nathan's grasp by running around the truck. In his haste to avoid Nathan's wrath, combined with the effects of recently smoked sticky green weed, Jorge tripped and banged his head against the Sixty thousand dollar Escalade. He lifted his head to reveal a small knot and an eye that would be seriously black and blue in thirty minutes or so.

Nathan turned to Sam and yelled at him for letting Jorge drive cars after smoking dope. He yelled at Sam for letting Jorge smoke dope on the job, even if he wasn't driving cars. He grabbed Sam's shoulders and looked in his eyes, demanding to smell his breath to see if they all had been smoking. Sam's breath smelled like curry, his eyes were clear and he was concerned. He was concerned that the situation could get totally out of hand. Sam wanted to deescalate the situation, douse the flame and avoid any violence.

A few seconds later, Jorge's buddy in bud appeared and Nathan's anger swiftly encompassed them both as they convened on the side of the Cadillac across from Nathan. The guy's name tag read Victor, his eyes were glassy, his speech was stuttered and his eyes revealed, as did Jorge's, that they smoked some bomb ass weed about fifteen minutes earlier. Not that Nathan had it in for any particular group, but in that moment, stoners were evil. Jorge was an evil stoner and was sporting a rapidly swelling forehead and the Cadillac had a small indenture from his head.

The day seemed like a completely bad idea to Nathan since everything had gone wrong so fast. He thought that perhaps he should go back home, climb in the bed and sleep it off, because tomorrow would surely be a better day. The current day was a bad concept, while tomorrow was ideal and even had its own pitch person in the form of an orphan named Annie.

If it could only be erased, replaced or removed, perhaps things would be different. Just as he was about to dive across the hood of the Caddie and grab the doobie brothers, a thought bubble appeared over his head. It was a sudden moment of clarity that could save his day; save his life even.

If he wrung the necks of dumb and dumber he would have opened a can of worms that should have remained closed. He could have wound up in the slammer with a bunch of "innocent" victims of the system, fighting for his life in an overcrowded prison cell. Perhaps it's not worth the price of admission, this fight that Nathan had been harking.

Maybe the best road was the one not lined with revenge or redemption. Perhaps accidents do occur and not all things are worthy of a blown inner gasket or bursting a blood vessel or even worse, a stint in the clink. If the day had been going bad, just wait until he was getting booked and fingerprinted down at the station Nathan thought.

Now that the moment had been firmly established and his need to pummel had receded, Nathan felt like a complete asshole. This was different than the mere asshole that he felt like earlier and definitely a lonelier place. What if the doobie brothers decided to turn the tables on him, Nathan thought. It would be two against one and the result could favor the home team. Nathan was sure that the garage was under surveillance, as most places were at that moment, and it's sure to be seen that he was angry, out of control and looking for a fight.

With the sudden clarity, Nathan decided to drop it down a notch but still wanted the wild and zany staff at the garage to understand how crazy he could get if his red Porsche was put in danger. So while in the moment of a rebel yell, Nathan turned to Sam and declared that his blood pressure has topped out and his insurance has lapsed and then walked away.

He headed down the same path that he ran up and was followed closely by Sam. Once Sam and Nathan were past the first bend, the duo of incompetence had gained strength in their misguided conviction that they hadn't done anything wrong and left the comfort of the Cadillac truck behind. They caught the pace of Nathan and Sam halfway past the first bend and cackled in the back like a bunch of Magpies.

Sam asked Nathan if he needed anything, perhaps a bottle of water or a maybe a cappuccino from the machine in the break room. Nathan responded nay with all the passion of a wilted plant. He tried to comfort Sam with the promise that he would not call the authorities on the venue. Sam told Nathan that he has two kids in college and insurance expenses for him and his wife that he's paying out of pocket and the glaring light of a court case could alter his existence. He asked Nathan if he was calm enough to work it out at the booth and Nathan nodded
Nathan, Sam, Jorge and Victor turned
around the second bend of the parking garage at the same time, took in the sight of the car and the garage together and all experienced a different reality.

Sam
"Oh shit, I've got a pile of customers waiting for me and this accident is gonna involve tons of paperwork"
Nathan

*"I can't believe all of this crap is happening to me and it's not
even noon"*
Jorge
"Why's this dude so angry, it's not like we wrecked his car"
Victor
"I've got the munchies for red Twizzlers"

Victor, Jorge and Sam headed for the booth to a gathering
of angry customers while Nathan slid into his car and restarted it.
He pumped the gas, dropped the stick to first gear and slowly
drove down the ramp. He pulled up across from the booth, turned
the car off and stepped out. The murmur of the crowd was quite
audible and the words would have been clear if the fog that
clouded Nathan's head wasn't so enveloping. Sam popped out
from the booth, grabbed Nathan by the elbow and led him to the
elevator. They descended one floor to the basement, where Sam
guided Nathan to the garage office. Once inside, Sam turned into
a completely different person.

Since Nathan made the mistake of informing Sam that his
car insurance had lapsed, the tables suddenly turned. Since the
leverage clearly rested with the garage, Sam started to dictate the
particulars of the arrangement. Sam said that the garage would
pay to have his car fixed by their auto repair vendor and that it
would take three weeks for the auto-body shop to make the repair
and return it to the garage.

He stepped over to the computer and pulled up the last
half hour of the garage video. It was a bit appalling for Nathan to
watch the out-of-control nut job spewing venom on the tape
because he was watching himself. Sam informed Nathan that the
surveillance camera on the top floor of the garage has been
broken for several weeks and that the video would paint a certain
picture of the whole episode.

The tape revealed that Nathan walked into the garage with
a combative attitude and that he was berating the staff from the

moment that they approached the booth. It wouldn't take much convincing that Nathan's abrasive and aggressive attitude, combined with Nathan chasing Jorge and pronouncing his intent to inflict bodily harm was the cause of the sudden appearance of Jorge's shiner and the knot on his forehead. It didn't look good for Nathan on the tape and with a bit of cooperation from the chronic crew, it would be a charge of assault and battery.

Sam became more emboldened by the minute as he watched the tape. He withdrew his earlier offer to rescind the parking fees for the next few months and stated that he didn't know how long it would take for the dents on the car to be fixed. His disposition was condescending, like anything that he offered to Nathan was a favor.

Sam knew that he had the edge, that he was sporting the upper hand in the situation. He knew that the last hour in the garage was the result of Nathan's anger. That he was working from the goodness of his heart to grant even an iota of compensation, via a free fix of Nathan's car, in light of the contents of the videotape.

Nathan thought that it was amazing how reality could be distorted by technology. Perhaps he should have wrung the dude's neck, at least then he could have vented the pent up anger that had returned to his body like a homing pigeon. If he was upset earlier, then his current disposition could best described as outraged.

He had been the victim of such outlandish behavior for the last few hours, and had consistently ended up on the wrong end of the deal. Each situation, starting from his encounter with the package in his office lobby and ending with the parking garage ordeal, delivered a clue that perhaps the day was jinxed.

Jinx, hex, root, etc; those were all words that Nathan discounted. He thought that they usurped one's own control of a situation and surrendered the outcome to outside forces. It was

alien to his beliefs and au contraire to the method of thinking that
guided him throughout his life. It relieved one from personal
culpability, which was always a cop out in the business world in
Nathan's mind.

It's never a jinx that a company didn't perform as
expected or that revenues paled to projections. That particularly
horrid day was the result of a handful of outcomes, borne from a
set of unpredicted situations and a lack of positive responses to
those unpredicted situations. Nathan felt it was his personal
failure to properly deal with the moment.
Failing to properly respond in the moment ran counter to a
defining characteristic of his existence. He prided himself on his
ability to handle difficult situations, which are always a bunch of
bundled moments. Not to spit shine recollection, but it was
abnormal for such a string of situations to arise that he
consistently failed at turning to his advantage. It gave him a
queasy feeling in his stomach, like the time he missed the final
question in the academic bowl in high school. The defeat was
more than he could handle, which made him stop competing
during his senior year, yet this was different; this was life and he
couldn't give up so easily.

That day started with an intent that differed from its
progression and direction. It started with his plan to meet Missy,
while avoiding the detection of his scandalous actions by his
loving wife Jackie. That day was supposed to satisfy his primal
urge to seek and conquer pretty things, yet it morphed into the day
from hell. To get any worse, he would have had to get stricken
with a disease of the worse sort. Not Cancer or any of the
inoperable, death assured variety, but the kind that would leave
him alive and in a helpless state, a few steps away from Jerry's
kids but without a telethon and throwback comedian to champion
the cause.

In a state of complete mental and physical exhaustion,
Nathan submitted to the demands of Sam the parking garage

manager and assured Sam that he, under no circumstances, would sue the garage for any damages suffered by his gleaming, red, Porsche machine. He would indemnify the garage for all dents, bumps, bruises and such that had marred the exterior of his vehicle. Feeling like a suspect whose will had been broken on Law & Order, Nathan agreed, verbally, that to speak a word of the incident to the authorities would insure the delivery of the damning tape to those same people.

On the way up from the sub-level office, Nathan was dragging his proverbial tail between his legs, feeling defeated and kicked to the curb. He exited the elevator and walked to his slightly damaged vehicle with the energy of a man who lost a war. He slowly drove his car out of the garage to the derision of Jorge, Victor and the rest of the heckling audience of people impatiently awaiting the delivery of their vehicles from the catacombs of automobile storage.

The rear view reflection was of the partners in pot, an audience of obvious Red Sox fans and a slow moving Cadillac truck, which looked like the one from the top floor. He pulled over at the entrance and ran back into the garage to check if he left anything behind. Like the proud but defeated general, he held his head high, checked the bench area and the booth for remnants of his presence and when all was clear, he strode back to his vehicle and took off.

CHAPTER 8

He turned out of the parking garage and headed for Broadway with his head swimming in confusion. His day, his manhood had been sullied by a cast of characters below him; below, even, the person on the bottom rung of the social ladder. He had been "punk'd" by, for all intents, migrant workers and it felt like crap.

A crew of recent immigrants punished his tantrums and ill behavior by negating his rights, but his tantrums were a product of their actions. Two Latin dopers, an over-leveraged Indian immigrant and a radical Muslim extremist had capsized his life and though he sounded like a complete racist, he totally didn't give a shit. The time for political correctness had passed, it's like he was at war with the whole city, one against many.

In the previous generation, a man in his situation would go home and beat his kids to relieve his frustration, but since he lived in the tabloid generation, he would get arrested for child abuse and make the cover of the New York Post. Besides, his little girl was far too young and precious for corporal punishment, so instead he drove on with the stigmata of abbreviated manhood tattooed on his forehead; accompanied by a horrible stench. He reeked of subjugation, of victimization and it filled the small sports car like bad cologne.

Though he felt like a bird with a broken wing, he couldn't wallow in pity and sorrow because he still had a full day ahead of him. He needed to cop a new shirt and then meet up with Missy for an afternoon rendezvous, which more and more seemed like the Holy Grail. It was turning into his trial by fire, though it started as his day's purpose. It was the energy that inspired him throughout the week and woke him up that morning. If he didn't meet up with Missy then he might have lost his grip on reality for a moment. He might have snapped since the only pay-off to such a day was the sweet smell that resided at the nape of Missy's neck

Driving the mean, red machine normally raised Nathan's spirits. It was usually an escape from the pressure and reality of his life. It could usually abbreviate feelings of emptiness and instill worth and meaning to his existence, but that day was a bit different. On that day, the drive complicated the whole thing. It compounded the ineptitude of the moment and shined a bright light on his imperfections. He felt like a man going through a mid-life crisis, even though he was only Thirty-Three years old, had all of his hair and was well endowed below the belt; or so he was told. He was feeling very fragile. Hell he might have gone ballistic if the traffic didn't start moving.

The ride downtown was actually anxiety and remorse ridden. Nathan felt like a chump in a gaudy red car. He was worked up and mashing the gas like an asshole from Connecticut in town for the day and heading to Scores. He was in a bubble of confusion and driving mechanically, not deriving the pleasure and excitem
ent imbued in the handling of a Porsche sports machine, which was a shame.

The legacy of the day had imposed itself onto the singular area that usually repealed outside interference. The one place that he could put behind the past and live in the moment. The vroom of the engine usually instigated a call to freedom that he naturally answered with a child-like excitement. Freedom from his inadequacies was generally guaranteed when the horsepower of the vehicle roared, but not that day. That day it only spotlighted the façade. The mask that he frequently hid behind could no longer sustain his false sense of superiority and it was eating him alive.

Nathan thought himself quite the survivor, though his survival produced a significant level of bitterness born from self-hated. He hated himself because he was a wimp, a man that hid behind a mask and that day it wouldn't pass mustard. That day he needed to assert himself and face his personal fears, but to do so in the moment.

It was many things thriving in Nathan's life. His family was going swell; well besides the fact that he's fooling around with fire by his rampant infidelity, which, was another example that he's weak. If he was strong, he would be content with his wife and daughter. They were quite the lovely family, fetching in looks and always fawned over by perfect strangers when out in public.

His wife was caring and affectionate, textbook issue "strong woman" that's behind every good man. His was the family to which men strove. It was the desired result of dating, dinners with awkward conversation and uncomfortable energy with different women. It's what drove a man to succeed in life, to have a beautiful and loving family, yet Nathan had inner demons that altered his perception.

Though hard to tell, especially since he went to great lengths to veil it, Nathan was terribly insecure and riddled with low self-esteem. He was a ferocious worker, quite cut-throat if need be and jumping rungs on the career ladder like a ewe, yet he still fought a daily battle with doubt. Doubts that he lacked what others had. That he wasn't smart enough. That he wasn't cunning enough. That he wasn't liked enough. That he wasn't handsome enough. In his mind, he was not enough of many things, though truthfully, it was quite motivational.

He worked harder, researched more, entertained longer than the next guy. Nathan felt that he absolutely needed to outwork and outperform to succeed in life and his superiors reaped the benefits. The old corporate dodgers at his firm recognized Nathan's insecurities right off the bat and understood, that with proper manipulation, the bright and ambitious worker with low self-esteem could be turned into a corporate tiger.

Nathan was quite invaluable and his position at the company was airtight. He lived in a splendid, classic six apartment. It was the type of place that he thirsted for while growing up, though once he attained it, he rarely spent much time there. Perhaps it was just a trophy for his mental mantle, a thing that he could point to when confronted with his insecurities. To top it off, he was pushing a lean, mean, driving machine, which happened to be slightly damaged.

The guesswork involved in determining if he would connect with his "self" each morning was like a raffle and often times he was unsuccessful. Often times he fell quite short and would soothe himself with his position in life and the little trinkets that he collected for moral support when he felt defective. Each morning, right before his first coffee, he would unfurl the mental checklist that he made the night before. He would see if his life was going according to plan and if not, what he could do to correct the course. His wife and his beautiful baby girl that cooed whenever Nathan's face came in her eyesight was proof of his success, yet he looked right past them and instead, chose to look at what he lacked.

That wasn't really a surprise, since he wasn't living in the moment at all. He had actually failed to live in any moment recently. He often conquered moments in business, but the personal moments were beyond him. Such failures were the downfall of many people, including him, and for the most part, they're never realized when at hand. It's probably because of the nature of a downfall, which is slower and more deliberate then a plummet.

A downfall is colored in neutral tones, while a plummet is fast, bright and intense. A plummet may actually have been better than a downfall, as the approach to rock bottom was swift and hence, there's a more immediate clarity of rectification or death and annihilation as the opposing options. Hell, a man can fall for years, twisting and flapping in the wind without self-awareness of his descent, which was Nathan's position as he pushed traffic to meet up with Missy. He's been in a downfall for many years and was getting close to the bottom.

He switched on the stereo from the steering wheel and tried to find his favorite Satellite Radio station, which didn't seem to have a steady schedule or perhaps he didn't have a steady schedule of when he was riding in his car. It was actually a real waste of money to have XM radio in the car since Nathan thought the content to be crappie, though the whole "satellite radio" thing was a real conversation starter with anyone riding on the passenger side. That actually made it worth the subscription price alone, though every now and then he would stumble across some really amazing music that would compel him to blast the volume and spazz out even after he parked the car.

When Nathan mashed the gas pedal, it was not clear to him that his downfall was beginning to accelerate. It wasn't clear that momentum was gathering like a penny dropped from a tall building as it neared the ground. If he could only realize that, perhaps he could save himself. The anger of that moment, or more succinctly, the preceding moments, raced his heart, though with no recourse in sight. He couldn't revisit the earlier events since moments can't be recaptured and even if so, he still had to meet Missy and didn't want to be late.

If he could revisit the moments from earlier that day, he would surely be all action. He would smack somebody around like a mafia flick. It would surely be the little old lady that spilled coffee on his shirt who got it first. To hell if she's old, she was young enough to buy a piping hot coffee and spill it on a perfect stranger, which qualified her for Nathan's "somebody's getting smacked" program.

It would surely be Islam the cabbie that got a smack, since his rudeness and lack of cab driver etiquette caused Nathan's blood to boil and caused his shitty disposition, which he proceeded to take out on the people at the garage. Without question it would be the whole staff at the garage and a few of the customers as well. He would save a double smack for Sam, the garage manager that went from being helpful to vengeful within a five-minute period.

Hell, he might have even smacked the perky sales girl at the Cingular store just for the sheer pleasure of smacking somebody, which Nathan had never done before. It made Nathan think that "smacking" was surely one of the most satisfying aspects of a pimp's job, not that he had any desire to be a pimp he thought to himself, while still harboring a bit of superiority; as if pimps we're dying at the chance to be Nathan.

He was moving very slowly with the log-jammed traffic and as he approached Union Square, it only got worse. He looked out the window and saw, what he thought, were throngs of carefree people that he vehemently envied. Not just the kids playing with their parents or nannies, but also adults who seemed to revel in the moment, happy to be alive. He rounded the bend and was passing Union Square Park, when a kid on a skateboard suddenly sprawled over the front of his car.
Nathan got out of his car as the kid skated off. Nathan called after him, but the kid simply looked back and smiled as he disappeared into the crowd of people. Nathan got back in his car and continued to seethe and curse that horrible day. He approached Fourteenth Street doing about 4 miles per hour and at the light, he pumped his engine some more, purely out of habit. It was a loud growl and startled an elderly woman that was passing in front of his car in the crosswalk. She shot Nathan a dirty look and he returned a menacing grin that showed all of his teeth like a wolf.

Traffic picked up after Union Square, which brightened his spirits just slightly. He popped open the glove compartment and rifled around for the bottle of Dior cologne that he kept there for emergency sprucing. He wanted to at least smell like a million bucks since he was looking like a Bowery bum, but couldn't locate the bottle. After a few minutes, he ducked his head to look inside the glove department while the car was still slightly in motion. He found the bottle and picked his head up just in time to jam the brakes and avoid hitting a Paris Hilton type walking with a man holding a snake around his neck.

They shot him a really dirty look and stood in front of his car in defiance. He blew the horn several times and gunned the engine while holding the car in neutral, which didn't make the odd couple budge one bit. After they felt that they made their point, the girl smacked the hood and screamed a few motherfuckers and then she, the man and his snake sauntered past and onto the sidewalk. When they stepped onto the curb and out of the sun, Nathan could tell that it wasn't even a girl, that Paris Hilton type, but a cross-dressing and petite young man.

It was a big city sight for sure and lightened his spirits momentarily. Nathan felt lucky not to be one of those freaks and found a bit of elitist comfort in the thought. He wondered what it must have been like to be those two guys, kind of ostracized by the public and only accepted by other freaks. It meant they couldn't go just anywhere and feel comfortable; they had to be around their own kind. They had to be around people that were equally as freakish and outlandish.

They couldn't just pop into Blue Ribbon late at night for lobster or fried chicken, or drop into Bliss Spa for a massage or a brief aromatherapy retreat. His centric mindset didn't dawn the thought that perhaps those two people didn't want to do those things. It didn't dawn on him that their lifestyle choice was just that, a choice. Perhaps they had their own places to drop into for late night food or a place to relieve a bit of stress when feeling the weight of the world on their shoulders. Maybe the Paris Hilton cross-dresser and the dude with the snake felt lucky not to be Nathan!

When Nathan drove past Eighth Street, he pulled his car over to the curb and hopped out. He was running really late and he knew that Missy was a fanatic about that. She didn't have a cell phone, which meant that he had to be on time when going to meet her. She hated that people were so comfortable being tardy since they could simply call ahead and announce that they were running late. He thought about that as he went into the wine store for a bottle of champagne.

Not that it was going to get him off the hook or anything, but perhaps it would cushion the blow of his late arrival and show that he was sorry for making her wait so long. She must have felt like a call girl waiting for him over thirty minutes in a hotel lobby, Nathan thought to himself as he perused the champagne section. He didn't want to get a bottle of Cristal Champagne, since it reminded Missy of an ex-boyfriend who used to keep bottles of it around like Poland Spring water. He was also leery of cheaper brands that went down fine but brought on a killer headache an hour later.

He settled on a bottle of Dom Perignon, which was actually better than Cristal and not as trendy, paid for it in cash and left the store. Halfway to his car, he decided to get her some flowers as well. He didn't know if it would be overkill but thought it better to be safe than sorry. Nathan asked the Mexican guy in front of the corner deli for a dozen of yellow roses wrapped in paper. Just as the man started to select his flowers, Nathan had an idea. He placed the bottle of Dom on the table and pulled out his blackberry.

He knew that Missy checked her email at the Apple Store on Prince Street and thought she might go there while waiting, so he composed an email message to her. Nathan said that he was running late for reasons beyond his control and that he really wanted to see her. He started to sign it "Love Nathan" but thought it was a bit much since he'd never said that he loved her before. It made him think about the topic a bit and he couldn't decide if he did or didn't love Missy. It was hard for him to clearly formulate what love meant to him, or better yet what it means to be in love.

He knew that he loved his wife, but he couldn't figure out if it's because of honest feelings for her or because she was his wife, the mother of his child and that he was supposed to love her. Not for nothing, but he felt that love was a tricky topic and one that's best left unmentioned until absolutely necessary! He pressed send on the message and when he looked back to the table, the man had already cut the flowers. He noticed that the flowers were wilting slightly and stopped the man from wrapping them

He was assured the flowers were fresh and had come in that morning but Nathan didn't want them. He told the flower guy that he wanted a new dozen; a dozen that he felt were fresh and smelled beautiful but was told that once they were cut, the customer had to buy them. He showed Nathan the roses before he cut them and since Nathan didn't have any objections, he thought they were to his liking. The flower guy didn't actually say it like that, but in his best-broken English conveyed that sentiment. Nathan objected and said he wouldn't pay for those flowers and was told by the flower guy that he couldn't get a new dozen.

Frustrated, Nathan gave the man the finger right in his face and then walked back to his car. Soon as he left the plastic covered, deli flower stand, he could see that he had a ticket. A fucking ticket! The fucking nerve of these people he thought to himself as he hopped inside, slammed the door and pulled away from the curb.

His anger meter had ratcheted back up to ten and he was beset with fury. He stopped to get flowers and champagne because he was late and he ended up wasting a few precious minutes since he didn't actually get the flowers. Suddenly, Nathan yelled out a bellowing scream, pulled his car over and jumped out.

He slammed his door and broke into a full stride down the block. He didn't wait for traffic and crossed the street as people blew their horns at him in anger. He streaked back into the deli flower stand and asked the dude for his bottle of Dom. His two hundred dollar bottle of Dom! Nathan screamed that he left the bottle right on the table and was only gone for a minute, so it should still be there. He then accused the man of taking the bottle and poked him in the chest.

In a few short seconds, Nathan had put the man in a headlock as he punched Nathan in the stomach and cursed in Spanish. Seconds later, three other Mexican men appeared from the store and joined in the melee, pummeling Nathan about his body and face with a flurry of blows. They all fell into the thick plastic and brought it down around them as they tumbled to the ground. In a scene right out of a movie, Nathan and the workers proceeded to roll on the ground, wrestle and punch though no serious damage was done since they were wrapped up pretty tight by the plastic.

The Chinese owner came out of the store and started to move his flowers out of harm's way. He pulled one of the Mexican guys off the top of the pile and started to curse him in the pigeon Spanish that many Chinese deli owners had learned to communicate with their employees. After the brief time that it took to move the flowers, the Deli owner and sole worker no longer involved in the melee started to pull apart the fighters. The deli owner said that he was going to fire everybody and have the damages taken out of their pay, which made the Mexican guys quickly fall into line.

Once it was broken up and everybody was on their feet, the Deli owner informed Nathan that he was calling the cops on him for assault and battery and destruction of his property. Nathan replied that the flower guy had stolen his two hundred dollar bottle of Champagne, which the flower guy denied. The deli owner pulled out his cell phone to call the police, so Nathan gave up explaining and took off running back towards his car. The thing had turned impossible and he felt like he had lost the day!

When he got right behind his car, he heard it making funny noises. It's like somebody was trying to drive it but didn't know how to work the gears. He got up to the car and opened the door, and there, slumped down in the seat with his foot on the gas and hand on the gears was a crack head. When Nathan jumped out of the car, he left the keys in the ignition which wasn't so smart in NYC. He grabbed the guy by the shirt with two hands and yanked him up out of the car and threw him into the street.

Cars swerved to avoid running over the would be car-thief as a crowd started to notice that Nathan was the guy who just had a fight at the deli and who also just threw the guy out of a car. It would normally look like a carjacking but the guy thrown from the expensive red car looked like a degenerate and asked people for money right where he was tossed. Still, it wasn't like Nathan looked like the toast of the town himself. In fact, he looked the part of a crazy man, wearing a stained and ripped AC/DC T-shirt with blood on the side of his mouth and nose from the dust-up at the deli.

He was pumped full of anger without an honest answer to the whole thing, his whole day and why it was happening. He was back in the red machine and headed to Soho to meet Missy. He tried to get her some flowers and it didn't work out. He never wanted to have her waiting down there in the first place, but he had car problems all day. Nathan was maneuvering the vehicle like a wild mustang as he drilled the engine and smashed the brakes a nanosecond later. It made the car buck like a bronco and represented just how he felt at that moment.

There was a strange bag in the passenger seat, which confused Nathan. A few more moments of the red machine bucking chucked a bottle of Dom Perignon champagne out of the bag like magic. It was his bottle, the one he bought at the liquor store but lost to the flower guy; or so he thought. He peered in the bag and saw the tools of a car thief. It was two screwdrivers, duck tape and a pack of skittles.

The crack head car thief must have stolen the bottle of champagne and when he saw Nathan run back to the deli, he tried to steal the car, Nathan thought to himself. This only made him angrier, made him feel like a conspiracy was amidst. It's like the whole world was trying to keep him from Missy, which gave it a sort of Shakespearean quality. It's possibly a tragic story of the heart and the forces that seek to stop the union of two people.

Perhaps the poetry angle was the first clue that Nathan was sliding off the deep end a bit. The situation started to consume him and eat away at the borders between a totally fucked up day and a four-scene tragedy. He looked in his review mirror and could see some people that he passed were pointing at him or his car or him and his car, which was what the Red Machine does for the driver.

But they were looking nervous and it looked like they were writing down his license plate number. Those particular people were doing their Good Samaritan bit and calling the cops about a man that beat up a deli staff, threw a guy out of a fancy Red Porsche with a slight bruise on the front, left side and was now driving it erratically down Broadway.

CHAPTER 9

Missy had been waiting in the lobby of the Soho Grand hotel for nearly thirty minutes and was tired of it. She stepped outside of the hotel and scanned the street for Nathan. She didn't have a cell phone and mostly communicated with Nathan via email. It wasn't an excruciatingly hot or humid day, yet she was sweating and feeling sticky. She thought how a part of the cell phone curse was that it allowed people to be late.

A simple call to the waiting party to inform them that they're running behind schedule and everything was supposed to be fine. It's also a luxury, since that ability to communicate could save the situation, though she purposely eschewed that luxury in exchange for the freedom from being constantly connected.

When she did have a cell phone, she felt at its beck and call. Whenever it rang, people on the other end expected it to be picked up. It's part of the social contract. It's the tyranny of constant connection and it sucked she thought. Several months ago, Missy lost her cell phone one too many times and decided that she wanted to unplug and tune out like the LSD experiments of the 1960's.

She decided to drop down to the lowest plan that Cingular offered and keep a voicemail on her phone explaining that she no longer had a phone, but did have voicemail. Technically, she still had service, but she was using it as a message center. She kept the number since it's been with her through thick and thin and her far-flung friends across the globe all used it to contact her. Unfortunately, it was the few jerks who still called that number that made her wish she had it disconnected.

Missy thought that the dedication and resolve of some guys were incredible. There were guys that she hadn't called back in months, but they still rang and left her messages like it was the first message. She explained on the voicemail that the simplest way to contact her was via email, which many of her local friends complained about.

Initially, she was the girl without the cell phone that always borrowed someone's cell phone to check her voicemail or make a quick call. She grew out of that in a month or two and became completely un-tethered……if one could actually be tethered to a cell phone. Though situations like waiting for Nathan in front of a hotel was when she wished that she still had one. If this were a hotel in Las Vegas, she would have been picked up for solicitation already.

Truthfully, she couldn't really borrow someone's phone to make a call because she didn't know anyone's phone number by heart. She debated carrying around a phone book for situations like this but never found the time or energy to write down everyone's info and felt that it was actually cheating on her stance not to be at the mercy of cell phones.

Though, if she could have simply called Nathan, Missy would have known what to do. She looked at her watch again, a thing that many of her friends no longer carried around since the cell phone replaced the watch as the de facto personal time piece, and decided that she wasn't going to wait anymore.

She went back inside the Soho Grand hotel and ordered a Mint tea to go and gazed out the window as the coffee barrister prepared it. She was thinking back over her life the past year and how it had been quite a roller coaster ride. She thought back to the men whom she chose to let into her life and the end result of those relationships. Most of them led to disappointment, with a few that really stuck out, but she thought that Nathan was quite interesting and wasn't sure what lay in their future.

She knew him for a several weeks but in the time since they met, he'd done a really good job of projecting his representative. The problem, as she knows from experience, was when the representative left and the real person showed up. It's no telling who that person would be. It could be a guy who turned out to be as quality a guy as his representative or even better and if that's the case, it wasn't really his representative that she met, but the real person who showed up from day one. That's rare though, Missy thought.

Often times the real person was quite ugly and someone that she wished she never met. She's been prone to ditch a guy before the forty-five day representative period ends to avoid the letdown of meeting the real guy. Now granted, she may have ditched a few dudes that were worthy of keeping around, since not every guy would pale in comparison to his representative or perhaps she had actually been with the real person, but for her sanity, she acted to preserve her heart and soul.

It could come across to guys that she's damaged goods when they run into her after she's fallen off the face of the earth, but what's the other option? Stick around in a relationship with a guy that she didn't like. She learned a while ago that you can't change a tiger's stripes. A man will be who he is regardless and any woman that thinks otherwise was fooling herself. The fact that she doesn't have a phone makes it even easier to deal with since they couldn't blow up her cell when she decides that it was time for her to exit, stage left.

It could also come across that she was cold and calculated when she left, but that was for a man to deal with and besides, men got over women quite easily, or at least that's what she told herself. It's usually the woman who slumped around for weeks, like she was at an Italian funeral, after a break-up. And the break up was usually because he wasn't who she thought he would be, or better yet, because he was a sneaky little snake that slithered around from woman to woman. Missy's been through enough of those situations and could honestly do without the headache and second guessing, let alone the derision of girlfriends who peppered her with "I told you so" at every possible turn.

It's not that she lived for the approval of her girlfriends, but the pain of a broken relationship, coupled with the post break-up chatter of chicks could send a girl on a downward spiral of premium ice-cream and Grey's Anatomy reruns for months; and quite frankly, she ran out of tasty flavors a few men ago. If she could at last find a guy who gave her hope that he won't morph into a creep after the forty-five day breakpoint, she could put an end to that particular compartment of anxiety in her life.

It could be that the type of man that she was attracted to was the root of her problems. She was either dealing with an artsy, good for nothing, slack ass or a silver spooned, obnoxious twit or even worse, a hungry, corporate ladder climber who looks at her as some sort of collectible for his fireplace. She really wasn't interested in any of those types of men in the long run, but she was ruled by her initial sense of whom she found interesting or cute. In the short term, it was fine and dandy. Things were sweet and the living was easy, but soon an ugly head would rear up and she stepped off; at least that's what she always thought.

Missy had a super fabulous Aunt, her grandmother's sister, that was a playwright and has been the bon vivant of New York, Los Angles, Paris and London, yet she had been unmarried forever. When Missy was a little girl, though she couldn't personally remember, her aunt Vivian was married for a year to a man that nobody ever spoke about. She Goggled Aunt Vivian and found that his name was Geoffrey, but could not find out any information about him. When her grandmother was on her deathbed, and Aunt Vivian came over from California, Missy raised the topic but was met with silence and empty stares.

In the back of her mind, Missy thinks that she may end up like Aunt Vivian, old and unmarried with a bunch of friends for companionship. Not to knock her aunt Vivian's arrangement, but she really did not want to go through life without a partner, a man that she could love, that would love her back and make her days special. It wasn't so fairytale to desire that. Though there are tons of strong women going through life without a man, it didn't necessarily make that type of life desirable for Missy.

She wanted the presence of a man she loved to form an unbreakable bond, a winning team that supported each other in a life that they lived to the fullest. Missy traveled throughout Europe several times but the next intercontinental excursion that she took should be with a husband or at least a man that loved her and her, him.

She had never been to Asia or Southeast Asia or Africa and what's the use of witnessing such beauty without someone to share it with, Missy thought. Gloria Steinem be damned, she wanted a man; hell, she needed a man and that's the truth. Missy went to the counter to pay for her Mint tea but realized that she needed to use the restroom before she left. She often left a place without using the restroom and then scrambled for a place to pee when she was in the street.

New York City was far from ideal when a public bathroom was needed. Popping into a restaurant or café and asking to use their bathroom merits the same treatment from the staff as if she went in to panhandle. Most places treated the non-customer bathroom user and the beggar with equal disdain, and placed signs forbidding bathroom usage by non-customers and begging for money right next to each other.

Missy pulled out a five-dollar bill and told the man to keep the change, then asked him to watch the tea for a spell while she went to the ladies room and disappeared around the corner before he had a chance to answer. On the way there, Missy remembered how much she really liked hotel bathrooms. They were always big and roomy, always smelled really nice and had many amenities such as sweet smelling soap, soft tissue paper and hand napkins along with sinks to die for.

The lighting was soft in the bathroom and when she looked in the mirror, she thought that she looked beautiful and that Nathan would be quite pleased with her appearance. She was giving bohemian chic, rocking a snug and sexy top with a flowing, ankle length skirt. Her hair was a mess of carefree curls that fell down to her shoulders and she wore just a hint of makeup. When she came out of the stall to wash her hands, she decided that instead of leaving she would go to the Apple store and check her email to see if Nathan sent her a message that he was running late.

She didn't want to waste the outfit and the moment of feeling beautiful, if at all possible. She got dressed with him in mind and wanted to give Nathan the benefit of the doubt that he didn't just stand her up on such a lovely summer day. She dried her hands with the towels bearing the hotel crest and gave herself one last look in the mirror before opening the bathroom door.

She popped back into the café to retrieve her tea and was met by a large group of tourists. She edged around to the service side of the counter to get the guy's attention but saw that the tea was sitting right there. She grabbed it, along with a few napkins, and headed downstairs where the doorman greeted her with a smile as he pushed open the heavy, wooden front door. As Missy strode into the street, mint tea in hand, she wondered why Hotel doors are always so heavy.

Soho was crowded with people enjoying the day and the street vendors were out in full force. Missy knew a few of the artist and vendors that worked the streets of Soho. She purchased a few pieces of jewelry from a designer on West Broadway and that artisan introduced her to several of her friends who worked on Prince Street. This meant that a leisurely stroll through Soho could take her quite a while.

She crossed the street to avoid walking in front of Cipriani, since her ex-boyfriend had lunch there quite often and she was in no mood to see him. She crossed to the east side of

West Broadway at the corner of Grand St. and headed up, towards Prince Street, sipping on her tea and ran into Marisol, the Argentinean jeweler. They caught up for a bit and Marisol told Missy that she would have some new pieces next week and that she would put a few pieces away just for her. Missy thanked Marisol and promised to stop by the following week. Any time after Tuesday was when Marisol said she would have the new items.

The tea was very hot and difficult to handle, especially since the guy at the Soho Grand didn't give her a cup holder. She had been gingerly sipping since she left the hotel and was getting impatient. She took a huge gulp and nearly burned a hole in her throat, which made her spit out some of the tea on the sidewalk as a family of tourist passed by and gave her a funny look. Missy started thinking about what she would do for the rest of the afternoon if she didn't see Nathan. Perhaps she could take a yoga class, though her favorite instructor was out of town and wouldn't return until the next day.

Near the Corner of Spring Street, Missy stopped to get a bag of honey-roasted cashews and then dropped half of them into her Tea. It was an old habit that softened up the Cashews when they absorbed the tea and sweetened the tea from the sugar of the honey-roasted nuts. Missy would drink the tea until it was gone, which would leave the cashews at the bottom of the cup. It could be perceived as being a bit peculiar, as a few of her friends had said before, but Missy thought that everyone had peculiarities.

Lately, she was so used to dumping guys that she's now a bit jittery about the prospect that Nathan could have dumped her. It's not that he had actually dumped her. In fact, it could be nothing more than an incredible set of circumstances that rendered him incapable of getting to the hotel in a reasonable time. As she was thinking that, Missy stopped in front of a store window to admire a beautiful dress made from colorful and delicate material.

She thought that it was tulle. Missy thought it was a dress that she would look stunning in, and made a mental note to come back to the store when she had more time. Perhaps when she comes to visit Marisol, Missy thought. Perhaps that dress and one of Marisol's new jewelry pieces would look great together at Claire's wedding at the end of the summer Missy thought and smiled.

Missy turned the corner onto Prince Street and headed towards the Apple store to check her email. The idea sounded far-fetched because Nathan knew that she didn't have a way to check her email while she waited for him at the Soho Grand Hotel. It was a very slim chance that he would send her a message; but she was at the store already so it was a moot point. She pushed through the door of the apple store and pretended to browse around upstairs for two minutes and then worked her way back down to the computers.

Missy couldn't help but feel embarrassed each time she went into the Apple store to check her email. It's like Internet freeloading, though the staff had told her that they encouraged usage of the computers. It was a great way to demonstrate the features of the computers and accessories such as the iPod and iPhone and it also helped the store to look busy. Still, Missy was always sheepish when signing onto Yahoo! to check her email or to check her Facebook page.

The wireless connection at the store was a little sluggish for some reason, and Yahoo! took a bit of time to load up. When it finally did, somebody named luckychic77 was the last person that used that computer to go onto Yahoo! Missy put in her screen name, msmissy16 and her password, which was the backwards spelling of her screen name, and quickly saw that Nathan did send her a message. She also saw that Claire, her favorite Yoga instructor that's getting married at the end of the summer, send her some sort of invitation.

The message that Nathan sent sounded as if it was rushed and quickly composed. She assumed he sent it from his blackberry, though he always makes it seem like it's coming from his desk computer. It apologized a few times for running extremely late and said that he would get to the Hotel in twenty minutes. The message was sent at 12:20pm, which means that twenty minutes would mean 12:40pm, and it was 12:30 when she read it. She decided that she wasn't in any hurry to scuttle back to the Hotel and perhaps wait another 30 minutes, so she opened up the email from Claire.

It wasn't actually from Claire but from her sister, Nikki, who was planning Claire's bachelorette party. Nikki wanted to get in touch with many of the friends and students of Claire but didn't have their contact information. Nikki thought that the best way to do that was to use Claire's email, and her contact list to invite everybody. It was supposed to be a surprise, though it could backfire quite easily, since everyone would have thought that the email came from Clair until they opened it.

Missy also checked her junk mail, to see if any good messages had been placed there. It was nothing but penis enlargement, penny stock and loan spam, and a few random party promotion emails. She returned to Nathan's missive and replied with:

Nathan,
I have a good mind to up and leave but it's such a lovely day that I don't mind waiting for you. I was in front of the Soho Grand but I'm now at the apple store. It's a good thing that I came here to see if you sent me an email or I would have walked away mad at you. I don't know what happened to make you so late to meet me, but you can tell me all about it. I'll see you at the Soho Grand, please hurry.
Missy

She inserted a smiley face emoticon at the end and hit send. She next went to her Facebook account and gave it a quick look-over before deciding to check it later when she had more time. She knew that Facebook could totally suck you in and before you knew it, an hour or two had been burnt responding, browsing and writing.

She went back to her Yahoo! account and signed out. It's been a few times that she forgot to sign out of different accounts while using the Internet at the Apple store and it bothered her for the whole day. It's no telling what someone could do with unfettered access to your email or Facebook account she thought.

After signing off, Missy went upstairs to check the price on an iPod speaker system, which sounded Hi-Tech thought it's really not. It was simply a device with speakers that an iPod plugs into. She was going to get it as a wedding present for Claire if the price was right and the sound was decent. She bought one several years back, when they first hit the market and it was a piece of crap. She had read that they've improved the product since then and she thought that it would make a great gift for someone that can't live without their iPod and Claire just happened to be that someone.

It's funny how people come into your life, Missy was thinking to herself as she browsed. She clearly remembered her first day of Claire's yoga class. Missy had recently returned to New York City from Venezuela, where she went for several months to stay with Nikki. She went there to cleanse the free radicals from her life.

Those free radicals were posing as people and causing Missy emotional and mental damage. Nikki and Missy became friends when they were both teenage foreign exchange students in London during their sophomore year in high school. They had so much fun learning, living and absorbing culture together, that they did it again, but this time in Paris for their senior year in high school.

Outside of the exchange program experience in high school, Missy and Nikki maintained a long distance friendship that was true and real. Missy would usually visit Nikki for a week each year and lie around on the beach and reminisce about London, Paris and about the other friends they had made in both cities.

They always stayed in touch through emails, phone calls and letters, so when Nikki sensed that Missy was going through a very rough patch, she suggested that Missy come down to South America for a breather. Nikki told Missy that everyone needs a breather from life every now and then, and Venezuela was the perfect place to do it.

She stayed down there with Nikki for several months and really enjoyed the beauty and pace of the country. The constant sun and sand and lovely dinners around a big table with Nikki's friends and family were especially enjoyable. She nearly convinced herself that she should move to Venezuela for good, especially with Nikki doing her best to make it so she would never want to leave. Missy decided ultimately, that she needed to go back to New York City and figure out her life and though Nikki was very sad, she understood. Her only demand was that Missy look up Claire when she got back to Manhattan.

Claire was Nikki's sister whom Missy never met. She was the sister that everyone spoke about in such glowing terms back in Venezuela. She was obviously dear to the whole family, especially Nikki, and often the topic of conversation over huge, endless dinners at Nikki's parent's house. Missy and Claire never met since Claire's study of Yoga and eastern culture led her across the world, though rarely back home to Venezuela. She was Nikki's older sister and quite beautiful in her countless portraits and candid snapshots that adorned the Inez household. The family resemblance was quite strong, with each sibling, aunt, uncle and cousin being a slightly different version of the same face.

When Missy got back to the states, Claire was the first person that she went to see. They quickly formed a friendship that had big sister/little sister characteristics, with a teacher/student dynamic as well. Missy was very interested in staying on a life path that would steer her clear of the pit-falls that previously meted her out a pretty sound emotional beating. She saw Claire as someone that could offer some guidance through her enlightenment, while also being her friend.

When Claire revealed that she just started a Yoga class, Missy was thrilled and quickly joined it. It's where she began the last big error of her life-Austin. Claire said that, often, it's the tumultuous road that leads to happiness and after hearing the whole story, she thought that Missy may have made the wrong decision; and Missy had begun to feel the same way. She had been recently thinking about Austin. She had been thinking about him quite often in fact.

Their relationship was very organic from the start. They knew each other already, but didn't really know each other at all. She had been back from Venezuela for only a week when she ran into Austin at Claire's Yoga class on the Lower East Side and from that moment, they were nearly inseparable. It was a relationship without labels and the time that they spent together was special. Missy felt like she came back to New York City and hit the Jackpot by finding somebody so right, so soon, but eventually, he turned out to be so wrong. He turned out to be the type of person that she went to South America to clean out of her life.

At least that's how she felt immediately after the incident at Marquee that caused the schism in their relationship, though she was having second thoughts about that night. Missy had been thinking that perhaps she was a bit hasty in deciphering the situation between her and Austin, especially after she found out that the Marquee incident was totally staged. Her former friend Jenny, who was in cahoots with her ex-boyfriend Dillon to sabotage her relationship with Austin, had planned it all out.

Jenny wanted to resume the BFF perks that came from Missy's relationship with Dillon and was willing to undermine Missy's happiness to do it. A friend didn't decide what made a friend happy, a friend supported a friend in being happy-unless the object of love was Heroin or crack cocaine, Missy thought. She had begun to see Austin as a lovely but lost soul that she was still attracted to.

She wasn't so sure when they were seeing each other and only after they separated did she realize she really loved Austin. He didn't actually cheat on Missy, if cheating was defined as sex outside of the relationship, though their relationship was never defined and lines weren't clearly delineated.

The time that she had been spending with Nathan made her think more of Austin and had confused her to what she actually wanted. Claire thought that it was selfish for Missy to leave Austin when it was obvious that what he really needed was support and love. It was clear to Claire that Austin was a bit adrift in the sea of life and needed some guidance. If Missy truly loved Austin, as she had been prone to telling Claire exactly that recently, in teary-eyed conversations, then to have left him for that staged indiscretion was a rather odd way of showing it.

Missy hadn't seen or heard from Austin in six months and neither had any of Missy's friends. She hoped that he was happy but she hoped that he wasn't happily in a relationship with another woman. If she were completely honest with herself, she would have admitted that she wanted to see him again and make efforts to restart their relationship, but she was just coming out of denial, albeit with a slow exit. It was the days when she was strolling around in the afternoon that the yearning to see Austin was the strongest. She always hoped to bump into him on the street, though she hadn't decided what she would say if she did.

Missy was thinking, perhaps, she would tell Nathan that she no longer wanted to see him. It wasn't the forty-five day rule at work, but simply that she needed to untangle the feelings in her head and heart and can't do it with Nathan, or any other guy in her life. She certainly liked Nathan and if he weren't running so late, she probably wouldn't have pondered the issue so deeply. She didn't start the day off with that on her mind. She actually planned a fun afternoon with Nathan, perhaps a midday romp at a hotel, but her mind had done a 360-degree turn. It made the rendezvous with Nathan difficult and one that she wasn't really looking forward to.

Missy snapped out of the extended thought and picked up the iPod stereo system that was on the shelf in front of her. She was consumed in the moment and in the midst of a cacophonous chatter of tourist from several countries. Missy looked at her watch and saw that she was running late. She thought about buying the iPod stereo system, but the line upstairs was long and the line downstairs was even longer. She put the box back on the shelf and made her way down the glass staircase and towards the door.

When Missy walked out of the Apple store she felt a bit of relief. She had a moment of clarity; an epiphany brought on by tourist chatter and computer humming, which freed her mind from indecision. She didn't know if Austin was still interested in her, perhaps he had already moved on in his life with another woman, but regardless, Missy knew what she wanted; and she was suddenly motivated to go and get it.

The blinding sun caused Missy to reach into her bag for the pair of shades that she never left home without. She slid them on and began to walk down Prince Street towards West Broadway. Missy saw a vendor friend on the south side of Prince and was headed her way. She stopped a quarter way down the block and was about to dart between the stalled cars when the traffic started moving again. She looked up the street and was about to cross when she gasped, because at the other side of Prince and Greene St. was Austin, or at least that's who it looked like with the sun bathing that corner in blinding light. She took off her sunglasses and squinted in that direction but still couldn't be sure if it was him. The light changed and she hesitated, not sure of what to do.

Missy hesitated because the person on the corner resembled Austin, but something wasn't right. If that was Austin, he had very weird energy about him. It was nervous and afraid and made her think about the energy of a suicide bomber on a mission. Not that she ever experienced a suicide bomber, but she could still imagine what that person's energy would be like. She lost sight of him when a group of map wielding Europeans walked out of the Apple Store and descended upon the corner. It was like a field trip from Finland enveloped the area, perhaps fifty people in total.

That was a serious pet peeve of Missy's; when tourists stood around in a huge group, blocking the corner and restricting the flow of pedestrian traffic. Pedestrian traffic trumps all else in New York City Missy always thought, and tourists, panhandlers and even vendors block the flow and are a nuisance. Even though they are a nuisance, Missy did like vendors and she tolerated panhandlers, but, and especially at that moment, she had strong disdain for tourists. It was those moments that a cell phone would have really come in handy.

The light changed for her to cross but she couldn't, something had frozen her in place. Her feet were leaden and her knees were weak and her eyes were functioning questionably. A particularly heavyset Finnish woman stepped to the side and there Missy clearly saw Austin. He had his cell phone to his ear and still looked quite nervous. He wasn't moving though. He was in cross mode, but he wasn't crossing; it's like he was waiting for something. The light had just changed and he stood pat the whole time.

He wasn't standing to the side like he was waiting for somebody, but was standing like a young girl about to jump double dutch rope, waiting for the right time to spring forward. The traffic started moving down Prince Street when Missy's line of vision picked up Nathan's car. It snapped her back to the moment, back to the fact that she was waiting for Nathan, who also looked nervous but more agitated.

He looked scarily agitated and his face was contorted and ugly as he stuck his head out the window and screamed some utterance that was drowned out by the urban soundscape. He didn't have on a shirt and tie as usual and was actually in a T-shirt that looked quite weathered. It was a look that she never saw on Nathan.

The confluence of Austin and Nathan on the same block, near the same corner was a jolt to Missy's senses. She spent the last 10 minutes in a blacked out mind vacuum, thinking about both men, how she felt and what she had to do, and suddenly they both appeared; together. Adding to the cacophony was a police car with sirens and lights a blazing, futile in its efforts to speed towards some emergency. The cops were stuck like the black Escalade, stuck like the white Mercedes Benz, stuck like, but probably not as angry as, Nathan in the red Porsche.

The honking of horns from gridlocked cars increased each time that the police car pumped its siren and lights. They were obviously in a hurry and Missy didn't understand why they would turn down Prince Street when traffic was at a standstill. They were elevating the traffic situation from bad to unbearable and within a few seconds, Missy heard another set of police sirens and horns. Suddenly, there was a break in the traffic and the cars gratefully lurched forward in a start and stop motion. Missy could hear Nathan revving his engine in a manner that perfectly matched his face and demeanor.

The Black Escalade in front of Nathan suddenly sped across the intersection and after a brief hesitation, Nathan followed suit, gunned his engine and burst forward. In the very same breath that Nathan's car took off, Missy called out to Austin, whose head swiveled slightly before he walked out into traffic and the front end of Nathan's moving car. With its low profile, Nathan's Porsche hit Austin in the legs, flipped him over onto the hood of the car and smashed his head into the windshield. Nathan slammed on the breaks as Austin rolled off the hood of the car and into the street.

The street cacophony hit a crescendo and then diminished to a semi-hush sans the incessant lights and sounds emitted from the cop cars. In the moment that Nathan's car struck Austin, Missy broke from her spot and ran towards the crowd that had formed in front of Austin's body. She ran into the fat tourist lady on the corner and spilled her green tea on a disgruntled homeless man. She knifed through the people and when she reached Austin, he was sprawled on the ground.

The car had a dent on the front bumper, the front window was damaged and Nathan was now standing outside of it with the door open, a look of shock and horror on his face. He closed the door and slowly walked over to Austin's lifeless body. When he cut through the crowd and looked down at the body in front of his car, he was surprised to see Missy cradling Nathan's head. The shock of the accident had turned his mind to a mushy gumbo, but seeing Missy there tossed him overboard, and he felt like he was in a bizarre dream. The surreal scene was unfolding in slow motion to the soundtrack of his heart beating double time. It was beating in his chest and in his ears.

Nathan and Missy looked at each other without saying any words for what seemed like an infinite amount of time. Missy had

tears rolling down her beautiful face and Nathan didn't
understand. He didn't understand why she wasn't comforting him.
He didn't understand why she was comforting the guy that
jumped in front of his car and caused the accident. He didn't
know who the guy was and why she was crying over him. Nathan
bent down and looked closely at Austin and could see that he was
still breathing. He looked over at Missy, who was still looking
down at Austin. She looked up and told Nathan that he was late.

CHAPTER 10

Suddenly, from out of the crowd came three police officers. One immediately bent down and tended to Austin while the other two grabbed Nathan and twisted his arm behind his back. Nathan resisted which made the officers slam him onto the hood of his damaged red Porsche. Missy screamed at the officers to leave Nathan alone while she sat on the ground as the other officer began to check Austin's vital signs. It soon turned into quite a scene with cops, an ambulance, stalled traffic and a crowd of onlookers. Soon, the EMS workers were tending to Austin and told Missy to step aside.

The cops questioned Nathan about the car. They thought that he stole the car since someone reported it being carjacked on Broadway, when Nathan had actually tossed out a car thief from the vehicle. The misunderstanding was par for Nathan's day. It's because he looked disheveled and bloody and surely not like the car's owner. His clothes were tattered and his face was battered, with crusty blood around the rim of his nose. Missy wasn't sure of what happened, but could see that Nathan was obviously in some sort of altercation on his way to meet her. She was just about to walk over to the officer and Nathan, when the EMT summoned her.

The medics put Austin onto the gurney and asked Missy if he was her husband. She said no and told the medic that they were friends and that she just happened to be in the area and witnessed the accident. They raised Austin into the ambulance but couldn't allow Missy to enter since she wasn't his relative or wife. The driver of the ambulance climbed behind the wheel while the other walked Missy over to the officer that was taking a statement from the Mexican flower worker and the Chinese deli owner. They had called the police and were driven down to the scene to identify Nathan as the guy that committed the assault at the deli.

The EMT told the police officer that Missy witnessed the accident and then began to walk away as Missy inquired about Austin's condition. He turned around and told her that his injuries were serious, but citing privacy issues, he apologized that he couldn't go into detail. The ambulance driver came over and told Missy that she could go to St. Vincent hospital on Seventh Avenue and speak to the front desk about seeing Austin, but that she should wait a few hours for him to be checked in and treated.

The police officer that tended to Austin told Missy that Nathan was suspected of carjacking, assault and perhaps motor vehicle assault. He asked if she knew of any previous altercations between Nathan and Austin, which may have precipitated Nathan striking Austin with his car. Missy told the officer that she happens to know both of them, but didn't think that they knew each other at all. The officer told Missy not to leave until he took her statement and then walked back over to the police car.

Nathan was handcuffed and sitting on the curb, right in front of the Apple store. His energy was weird, though that was to be expected based on his predicament. Missy was still thinking about Austin and concerned about his condition. She wondered if he was still unconscious and regretted not expressing her real feelings to him. She should have told Austin that she often thought of him and that she may have been too hasty in ending their relationship.

No, she should have said that she was way too fast in breaking it off and did it, partially, because the pseudo infidelity was so public, that peer pressure and pride guided her actions. As it would happen, tragedy struck just when she made the decision to reach out. Not to mention that the person who drove the car that knocked him unconscious was Nathan, which made Missy feel kind of responsible since Nathan was rushing to meet her when he hit Austin.

She looked at the car again and walked around to the passenger side window. She saw a bottle of champagne and a knapsack on the seat. The bottle of champagne made sense, but she thought that the knapsack definitely wasn't Nathan's. The accident didn't seem real to Missy. The officers had established that the Porsche did belong to Nathan but he was still in a lot of trouble for the assault on the Mexican flower guy and potentially auto vehicle assault. Missy felt sorry for Nathan and at that moment, she understood his energy.

He looked powerless, and Missy thought it was unique for him. She always saw Nathan as being in control. This new side of him was appealing to Missy, in a perverse way. She didn't think for a minute that he would have a problem with her breaking it off. It would hurt his male pride for a bit, which always happened with men, but no real emotions, or at least nothing related to him missing her.

A light bulb went off in Missy's head as she realized what was missing with Nathan. It was real feelings! The accident shed light on what she previously could not put her finger on. She didn't realize why it wasn't immediately apparent, which made her question her assessment of men.

Suddenly, Missy had another epiphany. Perhaps she was being to nostalgic about Austin, prettifying the memories through rose-colored glasses. He wasn't breaking down doors to see her. He hadn't called in months, not even stalking her apartment like a few other guys that she used to date. She went over to Nathan and sat next to him on the curb. She asked him how he was feeling and he gave her an empty look that spoke volumes.

Nathan began to ramble about how his day was ruined from the start. He said something about some old lady, a cab driver, a parking lot attendant and a car thief and apologized for being so late to meet her. The day was one long, successive fuck up and he wished that he could get a mulligan. She understood the feeling, as everyone has that horrible day where nothing went right, but unfortunately there weren't any mulligans in life. Missy wanted to do something for Nathan but didn't know what.

It appeared that he was definitely going down to the precinct and thought that perhaps she could go and bail him out. She couldn't accurately gauge how much trouble he was in, but gathered that his biggest problem was the assault on the guy giving a report to the cop. Missy asked Nathan if his tattered clothes and bloodied nose stemmed from the altercation with the Mexican guy. He said yes and told her that the Mexicans ganged up on him in the little flower nook in front of the deli, but that he was definitely the instigator.

Nathan looked like a hot mess and totally out of character. He was usually in control and the picture of composure. Missy couldn't envision Nathan with the passion and emotion that's necessary for a street fight or imagine anyone knocking him off his point. Perhaps it was all a facade and perhaps that facade masked uncertainty and weakness. Missy thought it to be an unfavorable trait at best. Not being unsure and scarred but the deception involved in masking it was unsavory.

If he was unsure and scared inside and was hiding behind cool confidence, what did that say for their relationship? That meant that it was based on emotional duplicity. Well, maybe it wasn't duplicity, but it surely wasn't the basis of a truthful connection between two people. Not that she felt she had that connection with Nathan anyway, though she felt for a moment that she saw something sweet in him. Missy's mind was drifting in thought when Nathan nudged her on the arm.

He apologized again, for being so late to meet her and for causing such a scene. Missy thought to tell Nathan that the man he struck with his car was the man whom she was in love with. That up until that very moment, she decided to break it off with him because of unfinished feelings for Austin. She didn't dare say that now. It would be cruel and uncaring. It would crush him to hear that and why kick a man when he's down. He was no longer

the cool and calculated robot but a scared little boy who had been
sent to the proverbial "Principals Office".

Nathan looked at Missy with genuine concern in his eyes
and began to ask how Austin was doing, or so she thought.
Nathan asked "how is" to which Missy cut him off by saying that
he was taken to the hospital in serious condition, obviously
referring to Austin. But what Nathan really inquired about with
such concern was his car.

He actually asked, "how is the car doing" instead of "how
is Austin doing" and right there Missy glimpsed another part of
Nathan. He didn't show remorse for hitting Austin. Showed no
concern that Austin was unconscious and in serious condition at
St. Vincent's hospital. He was concerned about his car!
She asked how he could inquire about his car before
inquiring about the guy that he struck with his car and she said it
with an indignant tone. It made Nathan question her level of
concern about the guy and not about him. Missy said that it was
only human to be concerned and that it was he whose feelings
were out of whack. Nathan recalled the image of Missy cradling
Austin's head in her lap in front of the Porsche and he asked why
she ran to that guy first instead of to him.

Before she could answer, Nathan writhed from a sharp
itch in his back and because his hands were cuffed, he was unable
to scratch it. He asked Missy if she would scratch it for him and
turned his back towards her. Missy obliged and as she scratched,
Nathan complained that she didn't seem concerned about how he
felt or that he had such a traumatic day or that he could end up in
jail. He asked in a joking manner if she would visit him on
Riker's Island and bring some fresh baked cookies. He became
more galling by the second, which made Missy dig her nails into
his back as she gave it a scratch.

Nathan screamed out that Missy was doing it too hard and
told her to go lower. The more he talked the more Missy disliked

him and thought that, perhaps, *all* of his true colors were shining through on this sunny afternoon in Soho. She was seeing him clearly and the picture was not appealing. Missy got to the lower part of his back as Nathan waxed on about her coming for a conjugal visit at the prison, when she saw something amazing. THIS FUCKER WAS WEARING A WEDDING RING!

Nathan could feel, in that same moment, that Missy saw his wedding band and he fell silent. They both sat their motionless for several seconds, she filling with anger, he thinking of all possible answers. Before she could speak, Nathan started explaining in rapid fire that he was married, but unhappily and that he was going to tell her today.

Before he could completely finish, Missy smacked him in the back of the head. He began to say that his feelings for her had grown so strong that it forced his hand on the matter and he was going to sit her down to talk about it when they met, but before he could finish, Missy smacked him in the back of the head again.

Each time that Nathan began to mount a defense for such a defenseless offense, she would smack him in the back of the head until he turned around to face her. Nathan had tears in his eyes and his lower lip was in the midst of an emotional tremble yet crocodile tears and histrionics were actually salt in the wound, as they represented his belief that he could hoodwink his way out of trouble. Without saying a word, Missy stood up and walked away.

Nathan screamed out towards her that his marriage was a loveless shell and that his heart was not in it, and said it with an award winning range of earnestness and angst. Missy walked back over to the curb and knelled in front of Nathan. She reached down in his back pocket, pulled out his wallet and unfurled a significant amount of pictures, and to Missy's further dismay, not only was Nathan married, but also the father of a beautiful baby girl. She whispered to herself how she can't believe that this little fucker was married and began her entrance into that catatonic, scorned lover state that marks the definite end of communication.

Just as Nathan was mounting his last ditch appeal, up ran Jacqueline, pushing the beautiful little girl in one of those expensive, privileged baby strollers. Her face was full of tears as she bent down to hug Nathan. Jacqueline said how she was so worried when a friend called her cell phone to say she saw Nathan handcuffed in the street, his car wrecked and blood and bruises on his face.

She hugged Nathan like she never wanted to let go, which was the true picture of how she felt about him and the state of their marriage. She loved him deeply and had been led to believe that it was reciprocal, when, tragically, Nathan only loved himself; if even that was so.

Jacqueline looked over at Missy, her eyes leaking concern and asked if she was involved in the accident. Without missing a beat, Missy responded that she witnessed the accident and Nathan was telling her how lucky he was to have such a lovely family and that he had so much to live for. Missy told Jacqueline that their daughter was lovely, folded up the wallet and gave it back to Nathan. She asked, to both Nathan and Missy, how such an accident could occur when the traffic was usually so congested on Prince Street in the afternoon. Nathan answered that the guy seemed to jump out in front of his car like he wanted to get hit.

Missy found that preposterous. Her heart welled up with fire and she was outraged that Nathan could even make such an absurd statement. She debated spilling the beans on the whole situation out of spite, but thought better. Why drag this lady through the mud in such a moment because of Nathan. She would allow Nathan to shed truth on the situation in his own way, but didn't want him to come out of this whole thing unscathed. He misled and lied to her, hospitalized the man she recently admitted to loving and then had the audacity to blame the accident on Austin.

She got up to leave, wished them health and happiness and took a few steps away, but then stopped and turned back around. She bent down to play with the baby for a few moments and then looked at Jacqueline. With the straightest face, Missy told her she would like to exchange phone numbers in case they needed her as a witness for the cops or his insurance company. Nathan tried to interject with his hands and lost his balance since they were still tucked behind his back and fell to the side like an egg.

Missy reached into her bag for a pen and a piece of paper and the wife did the same. The first thing she saw inside the bag was the back of a random business card that she had written Nathan's phone number on when they first met. She took out a pen and traced over his number as if she was actually writing it at that moment and handed it to the wife. Jacqueline was confused and visibly perplexed on how Missy had Nathan's number. Missy took the card back and changed the zero to an eight and apologized for her sloppy handwriting, though Jacqueline was still a bit perplexed about the similarity of the two numbers.

Jacqueline ripped a piece of paper out of her day planner, wrote down her cell number and passed it to Missy. She made a point to tell Jacqueline that the number would be disconnected in a day or two so she'll give a call in a week with her new one. Missy looked at Nathan after making the statement to clarify that he was not off the hook. Missy made it understood to Nathan, without speaking, that if she called his wife in a week or two, and the truth wasn't out, it would be out after their conversation. With that, Missy stood up, tickled the pretty baby one more time and then left.

She was trying to find the officer to see if he was ready to take her statement, when she heard a familiar voice call out her name. Coming from Greene Street was her ex-boyfriend Dillon, whom she had avoided seeing since her return to New York City. She accomplished that by avoiding places that were frequented by assholes; and since Dillon was an asshole she was able to duck him. Dillon ran up to Missy and tried to give her a big hug, but Missy blocked it with her arms. Dillon was aware that Missy despised him and she didn't know why he thought a hug would be appropriate.

Dillon asked Missy how she was doing and wondered why he hadn't seen her since she came back to New York. Missy replied that she was keeping a low profile and her life jerk-free, to which Dillon let loose with a big, inappropriate laugh, considering they both knew that Missy was referencing him as the jerk. Dillon told Missy that he was looking for Austin and asked if she saw him recently. Before she could answer, Dillon told Missy that Austin owed him three thousand dollars from a poker game and that he was going to take it out of his ass when he found him.

Missy found out about Jenny and Dillon's conspiracy at Marquee, where they planned it so that Missy would catch Austin in the act of cavorting with a gaggle of girls, so she figured that Dillon set Austin up again and this time to lose three thousand bucks. This, combined with Missy's basic contempt for him, led her to smack Dillon and walk away without looking back. She walked over to the cop who was still taking a statement from the Chinese deli owner and his Mexican flower worker.

It was taking longer than usual the cop said, because they all spoke different languages and the overlap of the three languages was small. The Chinese man understood about half of what the Mexican man was saying, and though the Chinese man spoke slightly better English than the Mexican man, it was still broken and made it difficult for the cop to write his report. Being surrounded by Nathan, his wife and kid and then Dillon was too much for Missy to deal with. She told the cop that Austin was her fiancé and that she really wanted to get to the hospital and check on his condition. It was a lie, but it was necessary at that moment. The cop told Missy that she still needed to give a statement. He gave Missy his card and allowed her to leave after she promised to call him the next day.

She walked to the corner of Broadway and Prince Street and hailed a taxi cab to St. Vincent hospital. The fracas on Prince Street backed up traffic in the area, and the cab driver was already complaining about it. He said that he almost had a fight earlier that afternoon with a passenger who wanted to be dropped off right in front of his destination. The traffic was so bad, that it made more sense if the passenger was dropped off at the corner. It would have saved the guy both time and money, especially since he claimed to be in a rush. When he wouldn't drive around the block, the guy exploded in a violent rage about it and wanted to fight.

After telling the story, he asked Missy if she would mind being dropped at the corner. He said if it was inconvenient for her, that he could go around the block to drop her right in front of the hospital, but that doing so would add extra time and money to the trip. Missy said that it was fine and understood. She hopped out of the cab two blocks away once it had become idle in traffic for too long. She paid the fare, tipped the driver and checked the backseat for anything that may have fell from her pockets or bag.

As she ran the few blocks to the hospital, she thought how Austin was imperfect with a pocketful of issues that he needed to resolve, but that she really liked him. She knew that she never met Austin's representative. She knew that the slightly dysfunctional person that he is was the exact person that she met in Claire's Yoga class. She knew that when she returned from Venezuela, she may have been too fast to pass judgment, too quick to purge from her life what she thought were pollutants.

The time that she spent with Austin was such a golden time that she found herself unsuccessfully trying to recreate it with other guys. She had initially minimalized his contribution to her happiness in the time that they were going out. She thought that her experience and new attitude were really responsible, but through the process of elimination, Missy saw the truth. She did that by sitting down and compiling a mental and emotional checklist of all the things that were and were not present in her life during and after her relationship with Austin.

She found that all the other non-Austin elements in her life were the same or had improved, such as her relationship to her body through yoga, her level of self-awareness and the constant cleansing of people pollutants that drained her energy. Since Austin, she wasn't as happy. Not to say that she had not been happy, but she hadn't been so happy and everyone deserved to be SO happy. When Missy arrived at St. Vincent's hospital, she saw the EMT that transported Austin and was told to speak with Ms. Hoffman at the front desk.

Ms. Hoffman was probably a lovable lady away from the job but behind the desk, she was not a happy camper. Her attitude had been soured by the experience of everybody needing something and needing that something right away. Ms. Hoffman didn't care that the people in front of her were filled with anxiety and fear or maybe filled with bullets; she actually didn't care. Years of tears and pleas to god for loved ones, combined with doling out procedural rigmarole day in and day out had left her with an icebox where her heart used to be. Ms. Hoffman was officially jaded.

Eventually, Ms. Hoffman let Missy in to see Austin, but since she never met Austin's parents, she couldn't reach out to them. She went by the hospital everyday to spend time with Austin, even though he was in a coma. She read to him and told him funny stories, which was widely considered to be highly effective interaction with a person in a coma. They said that a person could sometimes hear things while in a comatose state and Missy hoped that Austin heard some of the things that she said. Most of all, she hoped that Austin heard her say that she loved him.

EPILOGUE

The doctors said that he would come out of the coma soon, though a few days turned into a week and a week turned into a few weeks, and though the doctors knew what they were talking about, her faith had begun to waiver; if only so slightly. Missy didn't tell anyone about Austin being in a coma, even the few friends of his that she bumped into while he was in the hospital. She was stuck with the thought that he jumped in front of that car, which would make the accident a suicide attempt and she couldn't even try to wrap her brain around that idea.

Just as suddenly as the car accident occurred and induced the coma, Austin awoke one day. She didn't know if he had been awake for long or if he woke when she entered his room, but she went over to his bed and the conversation just picked up in the same manner that it picked up in their chance encounter at Claire's Yoga class.

Austin
"I thought you would had at least got me a better room"
Missy
"You were unconscious; a room is a room in that state"
Austin
"No flowers or anything?"
Missy
"You know you talk in your coma?"
Austin
"What did I say?"
Missy
"That you love me"
Austin
"Did I?"
Missy
"Yes you did"
Austin
"You got any witnesses?"
Missy

"Yup, half the hospital staff was in the room"
Austin
"Only half?"
Missy
"The other half was out getting you flowers"
Austin
"My head hurts"
Missy
"It should, you hit it against a moving car"
Austin
"Was the car red?"
Missy
"Yup"
Austin
"Wow"
Missy
"Exactly, you're lucky to be alive"
Austin
"What about my meeting?"
Missy
"What meeting?"
Austin
"Never mind; I thought you weren't talking to me"

Missy
"I changed my mind"
Austin
"Why?"
Missy
"Cause I wanted to"
Austin
"Want want want, that's all it is with you"
Missy
"Not that you gave a shit"
Austin
"I did"
Missy

"You never called or stalked my apartment"
Austin
"I did"
Missy
"No you didn't………………………Well I never saw you"
Austin
"I'm a great stalker, great stalkers don't get caught"
Missy
"You're a great liar"
Austin
"Thanks"
Missy
"Should I put you back in a coma?"
Austin
"Only if you can do it with a kiss"

With those words, Missy and Austin became inseparable! Again! He was released from the hospital five days later and convalesced comfortably at Missy's apartment for the next month. She waited until Austin was out of the hospital and then she called Nathan's wife. As expected, she was still under the impression that Nathan was the perfect loving husband and even after Missy told her, Jacqueline acted as if she didn't believe it. Jacqueline was content with her life and had a US military "Don't ask, don't tell" approach to the whole thing.

Missy would actually see Nathan every couple of months, out on one of his extramarital dates. It wasn't so secret anymore, as Jacqueline already capitulated to his infidelity and accepted it along with the lifestyle that Nathan provided for her. Either that or she and Nathan had an open marriage, though Missy couldn't imagine Nathan going for that.

In the end, the experience with Nathan had its value because it brought her back to Austin. That may not have happened if the series of events leading up to the accident never occurred; including the fateful initial run-in with Nathan at an art opening. Dillon totally moved on as well, though he still drunk dialed Missy's cell phone number at least once a month and left long rambling messages about nothing in particular. Missy thought that he just needed a friend as opposed to the Dillons that always kissed his butt. He had actually rotated in some new Dillons, a bit younger and more prone to actually have an opinion that was different than his.

Dillon could still be found at the hottest club in NYC or Miami or Paris, with an equal proportion of champagne bottles to half-naked women at his table. Austin never paid him that three grand and Dillon stopped asking about it after Missy threatened to get loose lipped on a few things that Dillon preferred to remain a secret.

Missy heard that Jenny and Nathan hooked up but that it didn't last so long. She thought that they would make a great couple, either Jenny and Nathan or even Jenny and Dillon, especially those two, since they worked so well together conspiring to separate Missy and Austin. Claire got married and Missy got her that iPod speaker system as a wedding present. Missy and Austin went to Claire's wedding, where Austin caught the garter belt and feigned as if he fainted.

Austin's been working more but still loafing a bit. He did design one of the hottest restaurants in the city, and landed that job as a trade-off for not suing Nathan over the car accident. The day of the accident was quite long, which meant that when Nathan ran into Austin with his car on Prince Street, he didn't have any auto insurance. So, if Austin sued, he would have attacked Nathan's personal finances directly, and that isn't how Nathan wanted the story to end. It happened that Nathan had a good buddy whose client was opening up a new restaurant and needed someone to design it.

It could be said that they all lived happily ever after, but fairy tales are soooo last year. It was a collision of people, both figurative and literal; it was a rendezvous with destiny.

THE END